CW00881664

Felicity Br
and the
Wizard's
Bookshop
Billy Bob Buttons
GALIBRATH'S WILL
Felicity Brady
and the
Wizard's
Bookshop
book 2
ARTICULUS QUEST
Felicity Brady
and the
Wizard's
Bookshop
Billy Bob
Buttons
INCANTUS GOTHMOG
Billy Bob Butto
Felicity Brady
Billy Bob
Buttons
book 4
GLUMWEEDY'S DEVIL
TOR
ASSASSIN HUNTER
TOR
WOLF RIS
book two of the TOR trilogy
I THINK I
MURDERED MISS
BUS
STOP
BILLY BOB BUTTONS
Muffin
MONSTER
Bob Buttons
the

BILLY BOB BUTTONS is the award-winning author of eleven children's novels including the Rubery Book Award FINALIST, Felicity Brady and the Wizard's Bookshop, the much loved The Gullfoss Legends, TOR Assassin Hunter, TOR Wolf Rising, the hysterical Muffin Monster and the UK People's Book Prize WINNER, I Think I Murdered Miss.

He is also a PATRON OF READING.

Born in the Viking city of York, he and his wife, Therese, a true Swedish girl from the IKEA county of Småland, now live in Stockholm and London. Their twin girls, Rebecca and Beatrix, and little boy, Albert, inspire Billy Bob every day to pick up a pen and work on his books.

When not writing, he enjoys tennis and playing 'MONSTER!' with his three children.

Mr. Longstreth

TIFFANY SPARROW

SPOOK SLAYER

BILLY BOE BUTTONS

The Wishing Shelf Press

www.bbbuttons.co.uk Twitter @BillyBobButtons
 1 0 9 8 7 6 5 4 3 2

ISBN 978 - 1522817338

Edited by Alison Emery, Therese Råsbäck and Svante Jurnell

FOR THE

GODPARENTS

CONTENTS

CHAPTER 1

IS IT KETCHUP? OR BLOOD?

MY NAME IS TIFFANY SPARROW AND my job is to slay spooks. It can be messy work, but I enjoy it. Mostly. I get to do a lot of travelling which is fun, but often just to crumbling tombs and spidery cellars. My mum was a Slayer too and so was my grandmother. I miss them terribly. They were killed, you see, by Grimdorf the warlock, so now there's only me and my old grandad left.

I live in Devil's Ash – delightful, I know – a tiny town in the north of Scotland. It is very, VERY different to most other towns. Here, ghosts linger on every corner, perch in every tree and lurk in every cellar. Over on Voodoo Street, there's a pitchfork-shaped park named after a highwayman who was hung from a tree there. I often see him on a wet night, huddled on a bench, juggling his eyeballs. He's a cheery sort of fellow, for a maggoty corpse.

Now I know to you, a 'normal' kid, all of this must seem very, VERY odd, but YOU don't watch TV being cuddled up to by the ghost of Henry VIII – he's so fat there's hardly any room on the sofa for me – and when you shower, YOU don't share it with a shimmering, slightly wispy-looking Winston Churchill.

YOU DON'T SEE GHOSTS EVERYWHERE YOU GO!

And I, well – I do.

My grandad, bless him, tells me it's in my blood. He calls it my 'wonderful gift'. But I disagree. STRONGLY! And I call it my 'ruddy nightmare'. If ever I ask him why it is only I can see them, he always says in a very lofty sort of way, 'A person who's colour blind can't see red, but red is still there.' And when I press him, he just clams up.

My grandad's that sort of person. You know, the sort who, if you ask him why birds fly all the way to Africa in the winter, he'll answer, 'Well, it's probably too far to walk.'

He's very clever, my grandad, but he can be very annoying too. And super-secretive.

Oddly, the only spot I never see ghosts is in the spooky cemetery on Bucket O' Blood Lane.

They must be hiding, cowering in rotten, silk-lined coffins, scared the Spook Slayer will find them and send them, well – to be honest, I don't know where. But wherever it is, they don't seem to want to go.

Now, don't get me wrong. I don't slay all ghosts. Just the pests, who think it's funny to skulk under children's beds or pinch toddlers' lollipops. The highwayman's not a problem – he only ever upsets dogs who want to play fetch with his eyeballs; yes, it seems dogs can see ghosts too – so I keep away from him; try not to stir him up. But there's a howling banshee in the Crusty Crypt Inn who's driving everybody crazy. He's top of my 'TO SLAY' list. And that, kids, is why I'm lurking by the door of the Hungry Skeleton Café on a moonless night. There's been a report of a spook in there who's up to no good and my job is to get rid of it.

The shop looks totally deserted, but I never go on looks. Too risky. This Monday, I popped in the Crusty Crypt Inn to pee and Genghis Khan's ghost was sleeping in the loo bowl. I wish I'd checked. I SO wish I'd checked. So now I pull out my silver compass and flip up the lid. Yes, just as I suspected. The arrow is spinning crazily. There must be a ghost in there; a big critter too by the look of it. Good job I'm fully kitted up in my steel-woven dress, my steel-capped boots buckled up to my knees. I check the Slayer tools hooked to my belt. Firstly, my skull bombs, just twist and toss. Three seconds later

BOOM!

They emit electro-magnetic bursts; very nasty on all things 'spooky'. Then, my pumpkin lantern, steel-shelled, the candle a potent blend of wax and gunpowder. Blindingly bright. And, finally, and most important of all, my trusty scythe clutched in my fist. It is called HELL'S TALON.

Its job...

To send spooks packing; and not to a cosy B

& B in Skegness.

All set! So, slowly, I creep over to the café. It is twenty feet back from the street, dimly lit by a flickering lamp over the porch. I try the door – well, you never know – but it's locked. I shrug and remedy the problem by elbowing in a window. It's cold for a July night and I'm in no mood to linger. Anyway, Percy Butts, the owner, he won't mind; he just wants rid of his spooky hooligan.

I climb gingerly in, dropping to the carpet with a glassy crunch. I sniff. It smells of burnt sugar in here, as if the spook I'm hunting is not so much the wispy leftovers of a person, but of an overly-baked choc-chip muffin. It's pitch black too, so I pull my lantern off my belt and switch it on. The café looks as if it had a wild bull for a customer: tipped-over stools, smashed lamps; and is that blood on the wall? With a nervy swallow, I put the tip of my finger in the red goo. Then I press it to my lips.

'Phew,' I murmur, ballooning my cheeks. It's just

Ketchup. With a sigh, I check my compass. The needle is now spinning with the ferocity of a wind-chime in a tornado. I'm confident there's been a ghost in here, but where is it now?

It must be hiding so, slowly, I go over the café foot by foot. Being mostly swirling light and a sort of gloopy goo – oddly, very similar to most of my grandad's cooking – they can shrink to the size of a tennis ball, so I look in the bin, the cashtill – it opens with a 'PING!' scaring the bejeepers out of me – I even check the pot of a prickly-looking, rugby ball-shaped cactus, but there's no sign of the spook.

I grit my teeth and sigh. I can't put it off any longer. The pesky ghost must be in the kitchen. Why oh why do they always go in there, I ponder crossly; a room full of pots, pans and rolling pins. Why not the bedroom? Then, all they can throw at me is a plumped-up pillow, a trashy Mills and Boon novel and a duvet.

Trying not to trip over all the mess – I seem to trip over most of it anyway – I skulk over to a door hidden in the shadows in the back of the shop. There is a tiny, oval window in the top of it and I peer in. Yes, there's the kitchen and, yes – SHOCK! HORROR! – just as I suspected, over by the oven, chomping on pepperoni pizza and surrounded by pots and pans (and a very hefty-looking rolling pin) is the ghost.

Hovering just a few feet over the newly-mopped floor, the wisps of energy shimmer and glow. It's sort of pretty; hypnotically so. But I know better. Through the foggy swirls I spot a short, burly-looking fellow in a bull-horned helmet and I think – yes, there is, there's a hatchet with a curved blade slung over his back. My chin drops to my chest. I remember him from my history books: the blood-thirsty eyes, the sunken cheeks, the perfectly trimmed hawk-like eyebrows. IT'S ATTILA THE HUN! What's the ghost of a 1,500 year old warlord doing here, in Devil's Ash? Apart from scoffing pepperoni pizza. Fretfully, I thumb the blade of HELL'S TALON. It is glowing crimson-red; it knows there's work to do.

Unsettled, I watch in disgust as a chunk of the pizza drops through the ghost and lands on the floor with a sticky PLOP! I find spooks often try to do the stuff they did when they were living: jump in the bath, scoff popcorn, even pop to the loo. But it never works. They just end up making a mess. But I think it helps them to feel better. Less like – worm food.

I switch off the lantern and hook it back on my dress. Now I've spotted the spook, I no longer need it. My Slayer blood is pumping through me. Suddenly, I feel sharper, no longer clumsy and I can see better than a barn owl. I drop to my knees and, very gently, push the door open. Keeping low, I shuffle in, working my way by a humming freezer and a glossy, steel sink.

Finally, I stop by a bin, the stench of rotten fish wafting up my nostrils. For a second, I hunker down there, listening to the ghost chomping on his midnight snack. Then I jump to my feet, levelling the scythe at the...

But the ghost is no longer there.

SPLAT!

A lump of soggy pizza lands on my shoulder. With a nervy gulp, I look up. There! Swinging from the lamp like a chimp. With a war cry, he zooms down at me.

'OH DRAT!' I yell, throwing myself to the floor. I roll over and over, bashing my shoulder on the bin and kicking over a mop and bucket, drenching my boots with mucky water. Then I jump to my feet. 'Now look,' I snap, rubbing my throbbing shoulder and glowering at the spook. I lift up my filthy left foot to show him. 'They were spotless.'

Suddenly, a frying pan hops off the top of the oven, thumping me in the eye. With a scowl, I finger the bleeding cut on my brow. Everybody knows a spook can't pick up and throw objects with his hand but, annoyingly, he can with the power of his mind. 'Listen up,' I snarl, as a rolling pin cartwheels over my red curls. 'If you stop misbehaving, you can stay in Devil's Ash. If you don't, I'll be forced to slay you. I don't want to but

I will.'

But over by the bin, Attila just hoots and snorts, enjoying his fun. He thinks he's a cat and I'm a ball of string.

Seeing red, I grit my teeth and advance on the chuckling ghost. Another even bigger, EVEN HARDER frying pan jumps off the wall and cartwheels my way, but I drop kick it and it slams harmlessly into the oven door.

Then – I'm on him.

With a wolfish howl, I swing HELL'S TALON. Attila pulls his sword, steel meets iron and the sword shatters. Steel wins! Slashing to and fro, my shimmering blade rips into the snowy swirls of energy. They wriggle and twist, crying for mercy. But there's no mercy here. Only when I'm tucked up in my bed do I weep for them, often crying myself to sleep. The spook grows slowly paler and paler, fading to nothingness; hand in hand, the steel in my fist dulls and the fury in my chest drops to a simmer, a pot of bubbling water snatched off the hob.

Then, from nowhere...

'HE HAS RETURNED!'

The entity's icy words echo in my mind, ricocheting off the walls like the howl of a banshee.

'Who?' I demand,

'You know who,' Attila whispers slyly. 'Grimdorf. He will slay the Slayer.'

'Grimdorf,' I mutter, my legs turning to jelly. 'I – I don't understand.'

But the last of the shimmering swirls vanish. The ghost is no longer there to answer me.

Slowly, I sink to the floor, my knees up to my chin. Grimdorf killed my grandmother. HE KILLED MY MUM! A volcano of pitiless fury erupts in my body. My chin snaps up, my jaws fly open and with untold ferocity...

I HOWL!

Later, in bed, my mind will not let me sleep. I tumble over and over on my mattress, my sheets bunched up and knotted, drenched from my twisting body.

In my tortured skull I see the moon. Then, just for a second, the shadowy walls of Lurch Manor. It towers over me, a horror film of filthy windows and towers capped in crooked roofs.

I see...

I see...

Cobwebs. Iron cobwebs. Hundreds of them, all jumbled up. Like me, they tumble over and over...

Suddenly, they stop and in my bedroom I lay perfectly still. Now, there is a low chanting. In my mind, I see a tunnel. It is blacker than the night between the stars but I can still see it perfectly: the low roof, the glistening icy walls.

Slowly, I creep up it. Skulls blanket the floor and, not wishing to step on them, I keep my eyes to my boots.

The tunnel begins to widen. The chanting seems to be everywhere now, crashing over me, drumming on my skull. But the words echo off the cavern walls and I cannot decipher them.

I know I must get closer.

I know only then will I understand.

CHAPTER 2

RUFUS SPLINTER OF LURCH MANOR

THE NEXT DAY IN HISTORY CLASS, I SIT slumped on my stool, elbows on desk, hands cupping my bony chin, my mind, well – my mind NOT on history. It is a blisteringly hot afternoon and, much to the dismay of my fellow students, Benny Flint, a boy who reeks of old tennis socks, is sitting directly in front of the whirling fan. The stink wafting off him is, to put it mildly, horrifying. But I don't smell anything. All I can think of is the spook I slayed yesterday and the terrifying news it whispered so slyly to me: 'He has returned. Grimdorf will slay the Slayer.'

The Slayer being poor...

old...

ME!

There's just no way, I tell myself, chewing feverishly on my lower lip. Just NO WAY! My grandmother and my mum were killed slaying the evil warlock over six years ago. No spook ever returns after being banished by a Slayer; never mind by two of the most powerful in history.

Now, there's no rule book for spook slaying; no list of DOs and DON'Ts I must follow. But, if there was, 'Slayed spooks STAY slayed' would be up there at the very top. Number One. Along with 'Never try to slay a spook on his or her territory' and 'Never, EVER pee on Genghis Khan's helmet'.

End of story. THE END!

I sigh a 'why's life so complicated' sort of sigh

and gingerly dab my left eye, still badly swollen from being hit by the cartwheeling frying pan. Grandad will know the truth. He knows everything there is to know on the subject of ghosts. He's sort of a library on legs. Old, crooked legs. I did try to talk to him yesterday night when I returned home from Spook Patrol, but he'd been asleep on the sofa in his study; and it's always so crazy in the mornings. But this evening, I'll tell him everything that happened in the café. Grandad will know what to do. He never lets me down even if it will upset him...

'Am I boring you, Miss Sparrow?'

I sit up sharply, thumping my knee on the lid of the desk. It bangs down, waking up the rest of the class. 'Oh, er – sorry,' I splutter, looking over at Mrs McGivern. One word best sums up my history tutor: Fleshy! Oh, and tubby. And rolly polly, blubbery blob. Her bottom is so big, it droops all the way down to the bottom of her knees. She is, to put it mildly, well-upholstered. Like a sofa. 'I was, er – just thinking,' I tell her.

'I see.' She screws up her lips in such a way they remind me of a cat's bottom. 'I'm on tenterhooks. Do tell.'

'Oh, er...' I try to think but it's as if my mind's a can of Spam and I need a tin opener to get into it. So I say what all kids say when they don't really WANT to say. 'Just stuff.'

A sprinkling of titters fills the classroom. I suspect most of them think I'm loopy. But they don't know me. They think they do, but they don't. If they did, they'd know I'm no different to them. I love ABBA songs too. And fluffy kittens. And films. AND I'm pretty good on Xbox – and Wii. But the problem is, kids meet up AFTER school, but by then I'm jammed under slaying unruly spooks. This Friday, Troy Crook – he's the super-cute boy I sit next to in French – is having his 13th birthday party. He even invited me. But there's no way Grandad will let me go. He's insisting I attend the Spook Slayers' Dinner. A bunch of crazy, old men swapping endless yarns and telling me how, 'In the good old days, spook slaying was just for boys.'

How dull!

Thankfully, the Spook Slayers' Dinner is only held when the moon is eclipsed, a fancy way of saying 'hardly ever'.

'See me when the bell rings,' Mrs McGivern barks, her three chins performing a jelly-wobble.

I balloon my cheeks and nod, a sharp jerk of my neck. I enjoy history. Mostly. All the inventors, the explorers and the legends of bold men dying for kings they had never even met. To be honest, I'm a bit of a history buff. But today, well – today I'm just not in the mood.

I try not to yawn. I never seem to sleep well, the spooks I slayed forever swirling in my skull. I see them on the backs of my eyelids, twisted and bloody. Full of fury, they yell, 'WHY ME? WHY ME?'

Suddenly. I feel the eyes of a spook on me. My blood pumps and, with a scowl, I twist on my stool. There! In the corner by the window, the chalky-white ghost of a boy in a tatty and torn military uniform. My stomach untightens and I feel myself slowly relax; he won't try to hurt me. I see him there every day, gazing gloomily out at the football pitch. But today, he's not staring out of the window. Today, he's staring directly at me.

For a long, LONG second, he just looks at me...

...looking at him. I think I see sympathy in his eyes. Even pity. Then he turns sharply away.

I keep on watching him. I often wonder why he looks so forlorn. I suspect he's simply fed up. It must be difficult sitting there every day, summer and winter, with nowhere to go. Lost and forgotten. I feel sorry for the boy but, still, I never talk to him. Grandad says it's best not to. 'Your job is to slay spooks,' he's always telling me, 'not to try to cheer them up.' Anyway, they detest me, even the spooks I'm NOT planning to do in. It is odd though, how nobody ever attempts to sit there. I think I'm the only person in here who can see him but everybody seems to inherently know the stool is taken.

'MISS SPARROW!'

With a gulp, I swing back. 'Sorry, Mrs McGivern.'

'I'm not interested in 'sorry',' she scolds me, her balled-up fists on her fleshy hips. 'But I am interested in you showing a tiny bit of interest in the history of this town.'

I nod. 'Yes, Mrs McGivern,' I mutter.

'Now, let me see...' She cocks her head like a wary sparrow – a very PLUMP, wary sparrow, '...oh yes! Devil's Ash is over three hundred years old...'

Gritting my teeth, I sit up and try to focus on the words spilling from her puffy, red lips. But there's a second spook over by the door – I think it's Sir Isaac Newton – who's trying to do ballerina twirls but keeps tripping over his frilly dress. It's very off-putting.

'...and the oldest dwelling is the mansion on the top of Ebony Hill. I was planning a history trip there but, sadly, it's derelict now and nobody's allowed in.'

My hands begin to tremble and I slip them under my knees. She must be referring to Lurch

Manor, the very manor I saw in my sleep last night. It belongs – or did belong – to Grimdorf, the warlock. Grandad warned me never ever to step foot in it. 'A nest of evil,' he told me. 'Fury even seeps from the cracks in the walls.' But, to be honest, I don't want to anyway. Not now; not after Grandmother and Mum were killed in the cellar.

'So it's empty?' pips in Jessy Cross, a tiny boy with spots and a crooked crew cut. I suspect his mum did it – with blunt clippers and an upturned bowl.

Mrs McGivern turns to the boy and rewards his interest with a banana-yellow smile. She must be thrilled to find a pupil who's not asleep. 'Why, yes,' she twitters. 'The owner, Rufus Splinter, was the town undertaker, but the town records show he was hung in 1703. It seems he had no wife or children so, with nobody to look after his home, it slowly rotted and fell to bits.'

Now I'm fully alert. Rufus Splinter was Grimdorf's name when he was just a man, just flesh and blood. Then, the day after he was killed and his ghost showed up, he'd changed it to Grimdorf. Nobody knows why.

'Who hung him?' asks Kitty Claw, a lanky girl with bushy eyebrows, who sits in the front row.

'The town.' Then, in a low, growly tenor, she adds, 'They say he dabbled in voodoo magic. They hung him for being a warlock.'

'What's that?' asks the girl, her eyes the size of dustbin lids.

'A sort of evil wizard,' chips in Jessy. 'They feed on tiny mewing kittens and keep scaly, three-eyed monsters for pets.'

Nervy titters fill the room. 'Stop being so silly,' retorts Kitty, turning to scowl at the chuckling boy. 'Monsters don't exist – and nor do wizards, except in books and silly Harry Potter films.'

'No, they don't,' agrees Mrs McGivern, patting the girl soothingly on her shoulder, 'but Rufus Splinter was born...'

'In 1666,' I mouth.

'...in 1666,' she says. 'Back then, if a person was even suspected of being a witch or a wizard, they were – ooh, how can I put this?' She frowns then snaps her fingers. 'Bumped off. Remember the witch hunts...'

'They burnt 'em all,' butts in Jessy with a colossal grin, 'till they were nothing but charred bone and teeth.'

She eyes the boy sternly. 'Yes, thank you, Jessy. Anyway, Rufus Splinter was hung on Thursday 31st October, 1703.'

'Halloween,' I mutter.

With a look of surprise, Mrs McGivern turns to me. It seems my mutter was a little too shrill. 'Correct, Miss Sparrow,' she commends me. 'On Halloween.' Then, with a quizzical frown, she adds, 'Do you happen to know the rest of the legend?'

I nod slowly. If Grandad was here, he'd tell me to say, 'No, I don't.' But he's not and, to be honest, I do love to show off, so, smugly, I inform her, 'Yes, it so happens I do. They say his putrid skeleton burst from the coffin and, in a swirl of red-eyed bats, it attacked Devil's Ash. It killed almost everybody. Men, women,' I swallow, 'and even children.'

Instantly, I'm the sole target for thirty-two sets of sceptical eyes. No, scratch that, thirty-three. The spook by the window is staring at me too. The twirling Sir Isaac Newton however, seems not too bothered. Shifting on my stool, I now wish I'd kept my trap firmly shut. Now, I don't suspect everybody thinks I'm loopy. Now, I know it.

But Mrs McGivern seems over the moon. 'Excellent, Miss Sparrow. Gold star. But remember, kids, it's just a silly legend.'

I snort. It just so happens this 'silly legend' is spot on. Then, three hundred years later, Grimdorf's skeleton returned to finish the town off, but my grandmother and mum stopped him. And they were killed doing it.

But I don't tell the class this.

THIS...

I don't tell anybody.

'I saw in the Quill 'n' Scroll newspaper they were planning to knock the old manor down, but they never did.' Mrs McGivern scowls so hard her face practically folds in two. 'I don't know why.'

But I do. The day after Grimdorf was finally banished, Mayor Hazzard sent a lorry and three gigantic, yellow bulldozers up there to demolish it. The lorry blew up and the bulldozers melted.

'My dad reckons the spirit of old Rufus is still in there,' pips in Jessy. He seems determined to frighten everybody in the class.

I rub my tired eyes. According to Attila the Hun's ghost, Jessy's dad is correct. But Mrs McGivern just laughs, reminding me of the yap of a startled poodle. 'Now there's only rats and bats,' she tells the class.

The bell rings and, instantly, everybody begins to pack up. Tossing my history books and a chewed Biro into my satchel, I sprint for the door, but a call from Mrs McGivern stops me in my tracks.

'Miss Sparrow! A word.'

With a drawn out sigh, I tramp over to her desk. 'Yes, Miss?' I prompt her.

For a long, LONG second she looks up at me. Then she slips off her specs and stands up. 'That's a very nasty cut over your eye,' she says. 'Hit by a bus, were you?'

She must be joking so I chuckle. 'No, I was, er – playing netball.' I put on my very, VERY best poker face.

'I see.' She nods thoughtfully as if I just told her a complicated bit of maths. 'So nobody hit you.'

'Oh no! Izzy elbowed me. Accidentally. She was trying to stop me from shooting. As if! Anyway, I still scored. And we won the match,' I add with a nervy titter.

'But Izzy's so much shorter," says Mrs McGivern, with a narrowing of her eyes. 'How did her elbow even...?'

'She jumped,' I interrupt her, mentally kicking myself. Grandad always says, 'If you must fib, Tiffany, keep it short and sweet.' So why am I babbling away like a fool?

'Miss Sparrow, think now, is there anything, ANYTHING you wish to tell me?' Smiling softly, she puts her hand on my shoulder.

I try not to flinch. It is the shoulder I hurt when I rolled on the café floor. 'No, no,' I chew briskly on my lower lip, 'I, er – don't think so.' I do not trust this woman. She seems the sort who, if I open the door and let her peer in, she will hop up on the sofa and put her feet up. I snap my fingers, 'I think Benny Flint shouldn't be allowed to sit in front of the fan,' I volunteer with a cheeky grin.

'This is not funny,' she scolds me. 'Every day, I see you with a new scratch or a new cut. A week ago, you were limping. Two weeks ago, you had two black eyes. They were so big I thought there was a panda sitting in my classroom.'

'That's a bit funny,' I murmur, trying to lighten her mood.

But she just looks sternly back at me.

I shrug and drop my eyes to my well-worn boots. What can I say? My job is to slay badly-behaved spooks and, often, I get hit by rolling pins and frying pans? Oh, that reminds me. 'Mrs McGivern, was Attila the Hun ever in Devil's Ash?'

She frowns and eyes me suspiciously. 'Why do you ask?'

'For my next history project. I need a character to study.'

'I see. No, he wasn't. Germany, yes, and most of Italy, but he was never in Scotland.'

I nod thoughtfully. How odd. 'Can I go now?' I ask her meekly. 'Dinner's at five and Grandad will be very upset if I miss it.'

'Why?' she snaps, her eyebrows lifting. 'Will he punish you?'

I shrug. 'Well, he might insist I swallow it. Grandad's a terrible cook.'

She rolls her eyes and slips her specs back onto the tip of her nose. 'Off y' trot, then. But if you do ever wish to discuss any, er – problems, just pop in and see me.'

'I will,' I mutter. Frowning, I snatch up my bag and plod over to the door. But there I stop. Slowly, I look over my shoulder to the back of the classroom. The ghostly boy is on his feet, his grey, misty eyes all hooded and sorrowful staring right back at me.

'Is there a problem, Miss Sparrow?' Mrs McGivern calls over.

But I pay her no heed. The boy just mouthed a word at me and, if I'm not mistaken, the word was 'RUN'.

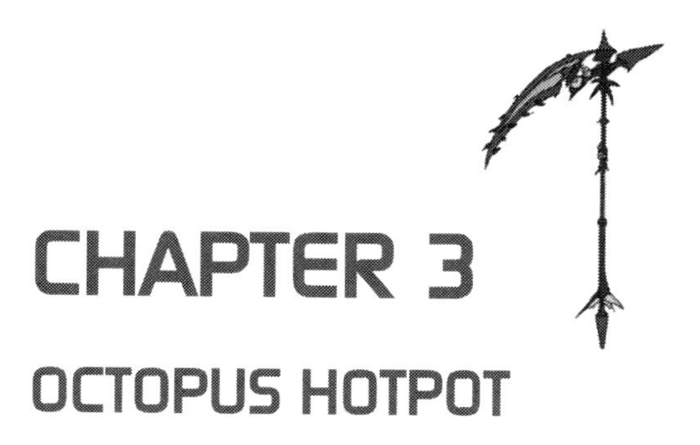

CHAPTER 3

OCTOPUS HOTPOT

A HALF HOUR LATER, HUMMING 'SUPER Trooper', ABBA's best ever song, I stroll up the cobbled path to my grandad's cottage. It is very pretty here, particularly in the summer. Honeysuckle sway in the weedless flower beds and a pink-petalled clematis clings stubbornly to the walls and seems determined to climb all the way up to the overhanging thatched roof. The windows look oddly tiny as if they were stolen from a dolls house and the worn front door is arched at the top and adorned with a

Wellington boot-shaped knocker.

Strolling up to the door – and by a very plump, opera-warbling spook – I look fondly on the old, rusty knocker. I still remember how much I'd enjoyed my visits to my grandparents, dressing up in Grandmother's lacy frocks, helping Grandad to feed his chickens. But, then, when I turned seven, Dad was run over by a drunk driver and killed and, a few months later, Grandmother and Mum were murdered by Grimdorf.

So I was sent to live full time with Grandad, here, in Devil's Ash.

Now, though, I never dress up in Grandmother's frocks and Grandad no longer has any chickens. Not that I don't love it here. I do. Grandad's the best; the best of the best – sort of. But I still miss Mum and Dad very, very much. And the chickens.

'Hi Gramps,' I holler, stomping in and hooking my tatty satchel on a peg in the hall.

'I'm in the kitchen,' he calls back. 'Grubs up!'

'Oh, okay.' My shoulders slump. 'But not too much for me,' I holler. Grandad thinks he's a master chef. He's always experimenting: eel stew, crocodile crumble, sheep's buttocks glazed with frogs' spit. In fact, it's amazing my poor bowels still work. On Monday he cooked octopus hotpot but it was so ghastly I tipped most of it into the pot of a weeping fig.

I smile evilly. I bet the poor plant's weeping now.

My dog, Boo, trots up to me and slobbers all over my legs. He's a Chow Chow, a big, fluffy ball of fluff. So much fluff, he can't see a thing which is why he's a spook too. He was killed when he picked a fight with what he thought was a much bigger dog. It was, in fact, a charging bull.

He lost.

Badly.

With Boo on my heels, I drag my feet up to my room, throw off my school uniform, toss it on the bed and pull on yellow shorts and a torn ABBA t-shirt. Then I plod back down to the kitchen to find Grandad thumping the metal sink with a badly-scorched, upturned pan.

'Octopus hotpot,' he enlightens me. 'But it seems to be, er...'

'Welded to the bottom?' I volunteer.

'Shy,' he corrects me stonily.

'Oh, I see.' With a roll of my eyes, I pull up a stool to watch the show, Boo curling up and hovering by my feet.

My grandad's a very odd-looking fellow. He always, ALWAYS has on a brown, patched-up jumper and very old slippers on his dolphin-flippered feet. His grey, wispy curls are hidden under a bobbly hat and he only has two teeth. Just two. He lost the rest of them in a cricket match. 'Mind you, I did catch the ball,' he always tells me with a playful wink. 'Just not with my hands.'

'Didn't we have octopus hotpot on Monday?' I ask him, crossing my fingers he'll let me order a 16" deep crust pizza.

'Yes, we did, we did.' He nods rapidly, banging the bottom of the pan with a wooden spoon. 'But you seemed to enjoy it so much. One second your bowl was full, the next it was empty.'

Smiling feebly, I glance at the withered plant by the sink. Yep, Grandad's food murdered it.

Suddenly, the floor judders and a jug of daffodils on the window sill begins to tip over. I grab it and stand it back up.

'BARK!' barks Boo, jumping up. 'BARK! BARK! BARK!'

'Fifth this week,' remarks Grandad.

I nod. Every day in Devil's Ash there's a tremor or even two but nobody seems to know why.

Everything in the kitchen looks old and torn, but I don't mind. It's still cosy. The wooden floor, scratched and dented, is mostly hidden under a tatty rug and, in almost every corner, spiders sit chewing on the wings of reckless insects. There's a rusty kettle perched on the gas cooker, the spout keenly eyeing the sink. I wonder, idly, if it is hoping for a dip and a scrub. I shift my bottom. The frayed padding on my stool is too thin and needs new wool.

'Gramps, can I shut the window?'

'Why? Oh, is it the opera lady? Is she still performing Madame Butterfly over by the snapdragons?'

I nod. 'She never stops.' I stretch over and unclick the latch. Instantly, the window slithers down and her nerve-splicing soprano is cut off.

'You know, if you want to slay her...'

'No, no,' I say swiftly, 'she's not a problem. I can put up with it.' With a thankful sigh, I turn to watch Grandad's ongoing battle with the octopus hotpot. I see it is now beginning to pick up speed. He slips a china bowl under it and, with a terrific thud, it lands there, cracking the bottom. With a nervy gulp, I wonder if my stomach lining will fare any better.

'After dinner, I think we'll work on your fighting skills.' I watch him transfer the grisly-looking mush to a much stronger, metal bowl. 'You need to be on top form for the Slayers' Dinner.'

'Why?' I ask him. 'It's just dinner. Unless you want me to karate chop a lemon tart.'

Chuckling, the old man plonks the bowl down in front of me. I eye it warily. The mushy-looking carrots and the charred peppers look sort of okay – they won't kill me anyway, but the twisty tentacle with the throbbing sucker on the tip...

'This Friday, you will meet every Spook Slayer in Scotland. Swiftfist Brent from Glasgow will be there, Jagger Steel, even Jub Jub and Cody Blitz. The problem is, they can be a little – playful.'

'Playful?'

'Yes, you know, boys being boys, fists tend to fly. So you must be fighting fit.'

'To stop them from killing me?'

Grandad laughs and playfully tweaks my cheek, a habit of his I find slightly annoying. 'No, no, they won't kill you. They'll just throw the odd punch, snap a leg or two...'

'Snap a leg! OR TWO!'

'Now, now, Tiffany, don't fret. Tonight we'll work on your foot work.'

'So I can run away?'

'Exactly.'

I balloon my cheeks. It seems, if the spooks don't finish me off, the other Spook Slayers will. Stiffening my jaw, I boldly smell the contents of my bowl. The waft of rotten fish shoots up my nostrils and I feel my stomach lurch. Luckily, if I do throw up over my food, it won't look any different to what's already in the bowl.

'I need a better name,' I suddenly blurt out. 'How will a Slayer called Swiftfist or Blitz or Job Job...'

'Jub Jub.'

'Whatever. How will they ever respect me if I'm

named after a tiny, plump bird with spindly legs and a fondness for worms?'

Grandad frowns thoughtfully. 'Interestingly,' he finally says, 'I was thinking of serving worms at the dinner. There's a tribe on the banks of the Amazon who...'

But I'm no longer listening. 'Terrifying Tiffany,' I murmur. Hmm, that's pretty good. Or Tiffany the Tigress. Even better! 'Gramps,' I interrupt his ramblings, 'the dinner begins at six, yes?'

Grandad nods. 'Six on the dot.'

'Excellent! So it will be over by seven thirty. Then I can slip off to Troy's birthday party.'

'Tiffany! This dinner is important.'

'Yes, I know. But...'

'No buts.'

'But...'

'Swiftfist's been slaying spooks for over half a century so, trust me, he knows a trick or two. If you stay till the very end when he's a little – tipsy, he'll probably let a few of them slip. Who knows what you'll pick up.' His eyes soften and he hands me two chopsticks. 'I want you to be the best Slayer you can be.'

'Why?'

'Tiffany!'

'No, WHY chopsticks?' I remember, yesterday, he'd only handed me a fork.

'Oh, er,' he flaps at hand at my bowl, 'I just discovered this dish is from Shikoku, a tiny island off Japan.' He shrugs. 'Anyway, it'll work your fingers a little; they need to be strong for picking locks.'

Boldly, I tweezer the slimy-looking octopus leg in the sticks and lift it up, eyeing the pulsating sucker with disgust.

'It took FOREVER to cook,' he adds, encouragingly. 'I even put a dash of frogs' spit in there, you know, to spice it up a little. It wasn't in the recipe but, I thought, why not? Worked well on the sheep's buttocks.'

I look at him in horror.

'But it was just a spoonful,' he adds hastily. 'Oh, and I remembered to put pepper in it too.'

My lips curl up ever so slightly; he knows I enjoy my food hot. 'Thanks, Gramps.' Oh well, it can only kill me. Agonisingly. In a pool of vomit. So I stuff the leg, pulsating sucker and all, into my mouth.

'Is it good?' Grandad asks, looking on hopefully.

But I can't answer; my jaw's cemented shut. With a monumental gulp, I swallow it down. 'It's, er – filling,' I gasp. If I ever happen to swallow scrambled rotten eggs drenched in pig poo this, I think, is what it'd taste like.

'So a B plus then,' he says, looking thrilled. He reminds me of a miser who just discovered a rock is a gold nugget.

'Er,' I don't want to hurt his feelings but I don't want him to cook it THREE days in a row. 'C minus,' I say tactfully.

'Hmmm.' He nods slowly. 'Well, a C's a pass.' And, with a chuckle, he tucks in too.

I prod at my food and wonder what to risk next, a mushy-looking carrot or a charred pepper. I drop the chopsticks into the bowl. Better to let my stomach cross swords with the twitchy tentacle first. 'Gramps.'

'Yes?'

'Yesterday, when I slayed the spook in the Hungry Skeleton Café...'

'Oh, yes! Sorry, it slipped my mind. How did it go?'

I screw up my nose. 'Okay. I think. The thing is, it was Attila the Hun.'

Grandad's eyes dart up from his bowl. I spot there is a tiny, green feeler dangling from the corner of his lips. He slurps it up. 'No! Honestly?'

I nod gloomily and put a finger to the cut on my brow. 'He lobbed a frying pan at me.'

'How rude.'

I nod in agreement. 'I thought so.'

Grandad chews thoughtfully on the octopus leg. 'Tiffany...' I know what's coming, '...did you try to help him?'

All innocent-eyed, I meet my grandad's shrewd gaze. 'Help him?'

'Did you tell him, if he stopped misbehaving he'd be allowed to stay in Devil's Ash?'

'Well, I...'

'Tiffany!' He sucks in his cheeks in annoyance. 'Your job is to slay spooks, not to rehabilitate them.'

I try to defend myself. 'But, what if, when they – you know, act up, it's just a cry for help.'

'A cry for help! A CRY FOR HELP!' With beetroot cheeks, Grandad glowers at me. 'Must I remind you of what happened with Zoltoff Snow, the vampire?'

'No,' I mutter sulkily.

'Well, I will anyway. If I remember correctly, you thought the bloody rampage he went on was the result of a rotten fang so you took him to the dentist. And what happened when you got there?'

'He bit the dentist,' I mutter.

'And where is the dentist now?' Grandad asks me loftily.

'Probably hanging in the church steeple.'

'And why is that?'

'He turned into a blood-sucking bat.'

Grandad rests his elbows on the table. 'Your grandmother always told me, the trick to slaying is to stay detached and to do it swiftly. A spook won't thank you if you try to help it. Remember, Tiffany, it's not murder. You can't kill a corpse.'

'But they yell and cry – and whimper.' I rub my left eye with a balled-up fist. 'It's just not much fun.'

He sighs. 'It's your job. Your – duty. It's in your...'

'Blood,' I snap. 'Yes, I know.'

'Well, it is. If Slayers stopped slaying, there'd be misbehaving spooks everywhere.' With a tut and, a little reluctantly it seems to me, he returns to his bowl. 'Well, let's hope old Swiftfist will drop a few hints on how best to dodge low-flying pots and pans.'

I nod. 'And rolling pins.'

'Oh, I forgot to tell you, he sent you a gift.'

Frowning, I sit up. 'Who? Swiftfist?'

He nods. 'I put it on your bed. Knowing you, you threw your uniform over it.' He pulls a hanky from his pocket and trumpets into it. 'Sorry,' he snivels. 'Bit of a cold.'

How odd. I never even met this Swiftfist fellow. Moodily, I play with my food, the tips of the chopsticks scratching on the bowl and wonder what it is. Then, plucking up my courage, I say, 'I don't want to upset you, Gramps, but Attila the Hun told me that Grimdorf...'

'TIFFANY!' he yells, jumping to his feet and almost upsetting his food. 'I told you He is not to be spoken of under this roof. Ever!'

By my feet, Boo jumps up too and growls. He's a very plucky sort of dog but, Grandad not being a Slayer, he can't even see him.

'Yes, yes, I know. I'm sorry Gramps. It's just, Attila told me He's returned.' I clench my fists and swallow. The thought of Grimdorf being after me is even harder to digest than the octopus hotpot. 'He told me He will slay the Slayer.'

'Poppycock,' barks Grandad, slouching back

down. His skin, I see, has turned whiter than lemon yoghurt. 'You know your mum and grandmother got rid of Him six years ago. No spook ever...'

'Returns after being slayed.' I nod jadedly. 'Yes, I know.'

Laying down his chopsticks, Grandad rests his elbows back on the table top. 'In 1703 that – monster almost, ALMOST destroyed Devil's Ash. But, three hundred years later, when he returned to finish the job, your mum and grandmother stopped him. They slayed the critter. Do you know how I know they slayed him, Tiffany?'

'Were you there?'

For a split second, the old man looks shocked. 'N-no,' he stammers. 'I'm no Slayer. My job's not to stop...' he sighs, 'that's not important. What is important is Devil's Ash is still standing. That's how I know. If they hadn't slayed him, he'd have destroyed this town, every brick and every timber, then and there.'

Steepling my fingers under my chin, I

reluctantly nod. There's logic to his words. But, as Grandad often says, I'm even stubborner than my mother was. 'Why, then, did Attila say it to me?' I persist. 'How did the ghost of a 1,500 year old warlord even know His name? I spoke to Mrs McGivern today and she told me Attila the Hun was never even in Scotland, never mind Devil's Ash.'

'That's impossible,' protests Grandad, scratching manically at his woolly hat. 'You know spooks only ever return to where they were when they were flesh and blood.'

'But what if she is correct?' I argue back. 'What if Attila the Hun, the man, never went to Scotland? Then how did his ghost end up in the Hungry Skeleton Café? And how is it Attila even knew Him?'

Grandad scowls down at his bowl and I wonder what's upsetting him the most, my blunt words or the fleshy octopus leg that's wedged between his two front teeth.

'You don't think He helped Attila to...'

'No, I don't,' he says firmly, refusing to let me finish. 'Mrs McGivern is mistaken. If it was Attila the Hun's ghost you slayed in the café, the flesh and blood Attila must have been to Devil's Ash. End of story.' He sighs, his eyes softening. 'But, if you wish, I will look him up in 'Devil's Ash, A History'. Excellent book. In there we'll discover not only when he was here but why. Better?'

I nod. 'Better.'

He looks at my brimming bowl and sighs. 'Not hungry?'

'No. Sorry.'

He nods and stands up. 'I admit it is a little, er – potent. I think I added too much frogs' spit.'

'But I thought you only put in a spoonful.'

'Well, yes, I did. A wooden spoonful.'

'Oh.' The tentacle in my belly is making a bid for freedom but I determinedly swallow it back down. Then I clamber to my feet and, with Boo in tow, I follow Grandad's flapping slippers out of the kitchen and down the hall to his study. There, I hum the first six bars of Incy Wincy Spider, the nursery rhyme my mum often sang to me when I was a kid. The study is instantly filled with blasting sirens. Up in the roof, tiny, red bulbs flash on and off, and bats fly off the rafters in panic. Then, with a 'FUUUUMP!', the far wall flips up and there, where the yellow, flowery wallpaper had been, there is now a dimly-lit room.

'In we go then,' says Grandad cheerily.

I'm in no mood for Slayer drills but I nod anyway and, with shoulders drooped, I follow him into the room.

Bigger than a haybarn, the floor is wicker, the walls thin and papery-looking. On a low bench in the corner there sits a bunch of skull bombs and pumpkin lanterns and, to the left of them, six dumbbells all lined up in a row. There is a map of Devil's Ash on the wall and, just under that, a brown, mahogany desk and a dressmaker's dummy. The dummy is looking a little dented, the result of being endlessly battered by my fists and feet.

This is SLAYER HQ, where Grandad instructs

me, where I work on my speed and agility. Where I try to be the best Slayer I can be.

I watch him limp over to the desk, the top hidden under a wonky hill of books. He always limps. A few months ago, when I asked him how it happened, he told me, when he was a boy he worked as a clown in a circus and fell off his unicycle. But I don't think he was telling the truth.

'Now, lets see,' he murmurs, pulling out the third book from the top. 'Yes, yes, here it is. 'Devil's Ash, A History'. Superb book this. Never lets me down.'

I decide to let him get on with it and begin to warm up. Fifty push ups followed by fifty jumping jacks. Then I snatch up the biggest of the dumbbells and push it up over my chest. Grandad must be correct. He always is. But, still, I worry. What if he's not? What if Attila the Hun, when he was a man, never went to Devil's Ash? Then how did his ghost end up here? I scowl vehemently at the dummy in the corner of the room. It's as if the key is hidden in my skull but I don't know where to look.

Then, in a moment of lucidity, a horrifying thought hits me. So horrifying, I'm frightened my curls will catch fire. 'GRAMPS!' I yell, letting go of the dumbbell and almost dropping it on my foot. 'Check for Genghis Khan too.'

CHAPTER 4

THE A TO Z OF LEMONS

TWO LONG, AGONISING HOURS LATER, I tow my feet up to my bedroom. I'm shattered from my work out, a back-wrenching, muscle-cramping mix of high kicks, jumps, rolls and jabs. Grandad even insisted I do two hundred and fifty frog hops! But it's not just shaky legs and battered elbows cluttering up my mind. Grandad discovered no record whatsoever of Attila the Hun or the loo-dwelling Genghis Khan ever being in Devil's Ash.

Finally, I left him half-hidden under his wobbly

hill of books insisting, in a rather hysterical sort of way, that A. I don't need to worry. And B. They must be in here and he'd soon find them.

But, deep down, I know he won't. Two spooks in a town they never lived in; never even visited when they were men. It's crazy! I know Grimdorf's responsible for it but I just can't work out how. Then there's the tiny, tiny problem of Rufus Splinter AKA Grimdorf. How is it he's here too? If he even is. My mum and grandmother slayed him six years ago and, as Grandad correctly insisted, no spook ever returns from being slayed.

It's a puzzle.

Stumbling into my room, I thankfully slam the door shut. I sleep in the loft. It is very cosy up here with sloping walls and a wonky floor. When my mum had been a kid, she'd slept in here too. Her tatty Enid Blyton books still crowd the bookshelf and Rebecca, her ragdoll, still sleeps in my bed. I see she is sitting up on the pillow, her left eye jammed shut so it looks as if she's winking at me. I pull on my slippers and wink back.

Ignoring the parcel Swiftfist sent me, I wander over to a stool by the window and drop down. It is still only seven o'clock and the sun is still up. I can see Grandad's shabby, old tool shed, the roof rotten and smothered in moss and, just by it, under a conker tree, a flower bed brimming with dancing snapdragons. The warbling spook is there too but, when she sees me looking, she grumpily turns her back on me.

With a shrug, I peer down at the floor. There, by my feet there is a pad and a wooden box. The lid is up, showing off a mix of pencils, a brush and six ink pots. The pots sit in two rows of three, a present from my dad on my 7th birthday. He even had 'Tiffany' etched on the lid, a flower climbing the leg of the 'T'. Suddenly, there is a second, much bigger tremor and I grab for the ink pots to stop them from spilling over. Why do they keep happening, I wonder, battling to stay on my stool. If they get much bigger, Grandad's tool shed will topple over.

When it finally stops, I put the paper on my knee, snatch up a pencil and begin to sketch. With a bark, Boo hops up on my bed; then, hovering just over the duvet, he curls up to watch.

With a sweep of my hand, the jutting stem of the snapdragon is drawn. I find this is the best way to do it; it is important the stem flows and is not jerky or bumpy. The top of the stem bows over to the bell-shaped flowers. Charily, I sketch the borders of the petals and pepper them with dots.

Drawing is how I relax. But, today, it's difficult. My mind is too full of Grimdorf. It is as if I'm standing in a street and, any second now, a cement truck is going to knock me over.

My sketch is now in need of a little colour. I unstopper the ink pots and dip the brush in the yellow. Soon Grimdorf is blanketed in much sweeter thoughts of snowy-tipped, yellow petals and green-speckled stems. Even the throb of my shoulder is forgotten.

I feel happy.

Content...

'TIFFANY!' yells up Grandad, his cry puncturing my happy bubble. 'Hurry up, will you. Soon by Spook Patrol.'

'I'll be there in a sec,' I yell back. Reluctantly, I stopper the ink pots, dry off the brush and rest the pad on the pillow to dry. Then I start to pull off my ABBA t-shirt.

'I'd stop if I were you.'

With a yell, I spin on my heels. There, standing by the door is the ghostly boy from my history class. 'GO AWAY!' I hiss, yanking my t-shirt back down. 'This is my bedroom. Strictly no spooks allowed.'

'I told you to run,' he says nonchalantly.

With narrow eyes, I leer at him. In school, when he'd mouthed the word to me, I'd simply ignored him and strolled off. But I didn't expect him to follow me back to my Grandad's cottage.

'What do you want?' I bark.

'Truthfully?' He says the word slowly. Perhaps it is difficult for him; a word seldom on his lips. 'I wish to help.'

I eye him distrustfully. My trusty scythe is three feet away, hooked over my bed. I step determinedly over to it.

'You know, most teenagers have a poster of a boy band on the wall,' he says lightly. He drifts even closer. 'Don't fret, Slayer, I'm not here to hurt you.'

I stop and put my hands on my hips. 'I – don't – fret,' I tell him icily, blowing a red curl out of my eye.

He grins mockingly. 'Yes, I know. I was told.'

I look him up and down and wonder who he's been talking to. Beyond the swirls of mist, I see he is thin and willowy, his body lost in a crumpled and torn RAF uniform, his hands hidden by the cuffs. There is a sort of waxy, buffed-up sheen to his skin as if he'd slept under a dripping candle, and, just over his left eye, I spot there is a jagged, red gash.

'Sweet dog,' he says, dropping down to pat Boo. Being a spook and mostly goo, he can do this; my dog being a spook and mostly goo too. But I'm not so, sadly, I can't.

Annoyingly, Boo seems to be enjoying his tummy rub. If he was a cat, he'd purr.

'What do you know of Grimdorf, the warlock?' he asks me bluntly.

I scowl and, inadvertently, step back. The name is like the call of a trumpet to me. 'I don't talk to spooks,' I tell him coldly.

He nods. 'Okay. Then I can't help you.' He stands up and turns to the window.

'Not very much,' I blurt out to his hunched-over back. Grandad always tells me never to trust spooks, but I need all the help I can get. 'I know he was hung for being a warlock and, the next day, his rotten skeleton burst from the tomb and attacked Devil's Ash. He killed pretty much everybody.'

The boy snaps his fingers, oddly silent, and steps up to me. 'Pretty much everybody, yes. Tell me Slayer...'

'Don't call me that.'

'Why? It's what you do.'

'But it's not who I am,' I retort angrily. I blink and my pulse slows. I can smell him now. Sickly sweet; the way all spooks smell. 'I don't call you Wormy Corpse,' I hiss.

He frowns, eyeballing me with the sort of puzzled interest a doctor shows when he sees a particularly nasty rash. Then, 'This is important. Why did he kill PRETTY MUCH EVERYBODY in Devil's Ash and not EVERYBODY?'

I think for a second. Why is this so important, I wonder. 'I, er – don't know.'

'Then think,' he snarls, her words bullish and sharp. 'A long time ago, the good folk of this town condemned him for being a warlock. Everybody, not pretty much everybody, EVERYBODY turned up to watch the hanging. The kids spat on him. They even threw rocks at him. Then, they stretched his neck. The next day, on Halloween, his skeleton burst from the tomb and went on a merciless rampage. Then, suddenly, he stopped. Why?'

'He left the oven on?' I suggest lamely.

He rolls his eyes and tuts.

'Is he back then?' I venture. 'The other day, a spook told me...'

'Attila the Hun,' he interrupts me with a knowing nod. 'Yes, I know. And, yes, he is.'

'But – but he can't be,' I splutter in palpable dismay. I can't be killed; I'm only thirteen!

'Well, he is. It's not important what you think. If he's here, he's here.'

'Flippin' heck,' I murmur, feeling thoroughly fed up. Now I'm in the poo.

'I have bad news,' the boy says.

'That WAS bad news,' I retort hotly.

'Well, this is terrible news then. It's not just him.'

'It's not?'

'No.'

'Well, who's with him? His Mum? His dentist?'

'An army.'

'An army!'

'Of spooks.'

'OF SPOOKS!' My words judder and pitch, from

soprano to a deep tenor. I feel so numb I wonder how I can possibly exist.

'And not any old spooks. Monsters. From history. Hundreds of them.'

'Hundreds!' I whimper. I mustn't cry. I mustn't cry.

'You know, if you ever give up being a Slayer, you'd make a wonderful echo.'

Through my fog of self pity, I shoot him a withering look. Why is life so difficult? It's like trying to run in one of my Grandad's stews. 'But why?' I muster. 'And how did Grimdorf get them here? And how did he return after being slayed by TWO Slayers?'

He chomps for a second on his lower lip. I can almost see the cogs in his skull twirling. 'But you and I know that's impossible.' He says this very slowly, as if he's talking to a toddler.

'Yes, I know,' I hiss, inflamed by his patronising tone. 'So?'

He rolls his eyes, annoying me further. 'Listen, Slayer...'

'Don't call me...'

'Listen! If it's impossible for him to return but he still did, then...'

A light bulb flickers on in my skull. 'Oh no,' I muster pitifully, gazing at the floor. I wonder if there's a book, 'The A to Z of Lemons', and I'm in there under 'T'. Slowly, I look up at the boy. 'My mum and grandmother never slayed him, did they?'

'Finally!'

My mind is a jumble, the thump in my chest lopsided like a one-man band. 'But...'

'No buts,' he snaps, reminding me of my grandad, He begins to glide over to my bedroom window. 'Just try to discover why Grimdorf did not destroy ALL of Devil's Ash back in 1703. If you can do that, you'll be a step closer.'

'A step closer to what?'

He looks back at me, his eyebrows arched hawkishly. 'To stopping him murdering you, Stupid.'

I feel my jaw harden. 'Why don't you just tell

me?' I storm.

'Tell you! Now where's the sport in that?' Then, with a twitch of his lips, he adds, 'Ask your old grandad who Imelda Cartwright is?'

'Who?'

He shoots me with his index finger. 'Exactly.'

I frown. Why, I wonder is he trying to help me. What's in it for him? And why do I suddenly feel so crushingly stupid? 'What's your name?' I suddenly ask him.

He shrugs. 'Just call me Wormy Corpse,' he says evenly. Then, with a cheeky wink, he drifts through the glass.

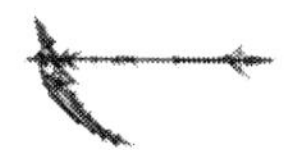

It is almost two o'clock in the morning but I simply cannot sleep. I was forced to slay two spooks this night – the howling banshee in the Crust Crypt Inn and a letter-munching blob hiding in a post box - and the yells still bother me. I'm hungry too and, over by the window, there is a rat, his tiny, scampering paws drumming on my skull, unnerving me.

In my muddled, sleep-robbed mind, I see a jumble of dusty, cobwebby rooms; then, a second later, a tangled forest of gnarled trees. The tunnel is there too, the chanting still muffled, echoing off the roof and the icy walls.

Keen to decipher the words, I hurry up the tunnel, yellow-tarnished skulls splintering under my boots, till, finally, I find myself in a gigantic cavern.

I swallow. It is crowded with hooded spooks; rows upon rows of them like troops on parade. Over and over they chant...

They chant...

I scowl; the echo in the room is awful. It is too difficult to...

Clickety click. Clickety click. Clickety click. The rat is driving me crazy!

In a flurry of pillows and tangled blankets, I hop up off my bed and march over to the window, but the annoying rodent is nowhere to be seen.

Slamming my fist on the wallpaper, I look out at the street. The moon, I see, is full, draping a lazy glow over the flower beds and Grandad's old tool shed. There, on the shed's roof, I spot a ghostly cat, but over by the path the opera-warbling spook is nowhere to be seen.

Which is odd.

She's always there!

The wind too cannot sleep, tossing in her bed, knocking the conkers off the...

Then, I see him.

GRIMDORF!

His black eyes crackling and sparking as if he'd swallowed a thunder cloud. His cheeks swarming with tiny maggots. His crocodile teeth erupting from car-crusher sized jaws.

A burst of red-hot fury thumps me in the chest and, with a cry, I sink to the floor, my knees to my chin. Curled up like a baby in a womb, I pray for it to stop. I WILL DO ANYTHING! ANYTHING IF IT WILL JUST STOP.

'Now, that is interesting,' the demon in my mind rasps slyly.

CHAPTER 5

MONSTER BALL

A sky bulging, soon to burst,
A growl of thunder over a manor cursed,
A trumpet call, shrill and strong,
Calling out to the worm-ridden throng,
Cannons BOOM! They crowd in like sheep,
A howling pack, a hundred deep.

No giggling girls, no well-groomed men,
Only monsters creep in this den,
Bullish grunts and rasping growls,
A rock band plays and a banshee howls,
A powerful wizard is the skeletal host,
To a ballroom packed with dusty ghosts.

Grimdorf slumps on a red-jewelled throne,
No skin, no flesh, just brittle bone,
He leers down at the bopping mob,
Yes, he thinks, they'll do the job.
'Soon, y' rotters, we'll destroy this town,
But first, hurry up and chug this down.'

In his fist, a bottle, stoppered with poop,
Filled to the brim with bubbling gloop,
'This,' he barks, 'will stop the rot,
Chests will throb, will thump TICK TOCK!'
A drooling yeti fights to be first,
With a victory sneer, Grimdorf feeds the cursed.

He sniggers, watching his plan unfold,
Then he calls to a mummy swathed in mold,
With a howl, the yeti stomps over too,
They sit and bicker, who will murder who,
'Just kill the Slayer,' Grimdorf grunts,
The yeti nods and sets off to hunt.

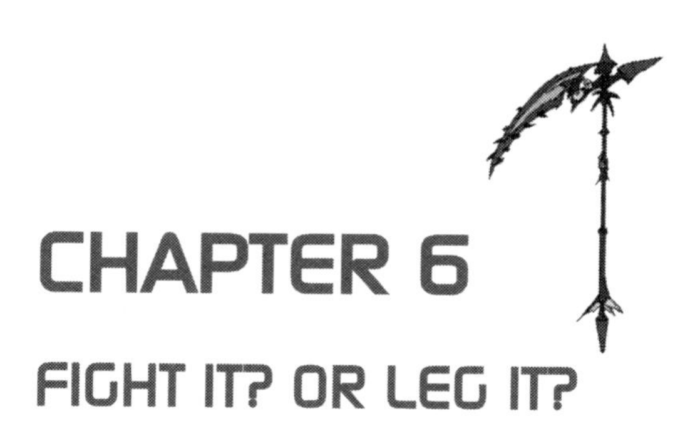

CHAPTER 6

FIGHT IT? OR LEG IT?

WITH THE BLURRY EYES OF A person woken up by a bucket of icy water, I creep over to the door of the Murder Ink bookshop and, very softly, press my fingertips to the mildewed wood. My eyebrows lift as it springs open. I'd sort of expected it to be locked.

I blink the sleep from my eyes and glance at my watch. It is three o'clock in the morning so it is still dark out, the sky inky black with just a splash of cloud and dots of stars. There's been a report of 'HOWLING' in the shop so Grandad prodded me till I woke up and, after a brimming bowl of Sugarpuffs, sent me to check it out. Normally, I'd be pretty upset at being dragged from my bed at such a crazy hour, but tonight it's not a problem. After spotting Grimdorf lurking in the flower bed, I'm hardly in the mood to sleep.

I check my compass and see, to my surprise, that the silver needle is perfectly still. I look closer and gulp. The tip of the needle has melted and is welded to the glass casing.

The walky-talky on my belt begins to judder and beep. 'Control to Tiffany. What's your status, over?'

It's Grandad.

I almost never bother to bring my walky-talky with me on Spook Patrol. I find it too distracting. But, tonight, Grandad insisted, In fact, he seemed pretty twitchy when I left. I think it upset him when he didn't find any record of Hun or Khan in his 'never lets me down' history book.

With a long, LOOONG sigh, I snatch the

convulsing box off my belt and put it to my lips. 'I can't see anything from the street,' I tell him. 'The window's too dirty. But the door's unlocked so I'm going in for a look see.'

A crackly silence greets my words.

I roll my eyes. 'Over,' I hiss. Grandad insists on 'PROPER PROTOCOL' when I'm using my walky-talky. I think he thinks he's 'M' and I'm '007'. It's super annoying.

'Understood,' he responds. 'But keep your eyes peeled. It might be a trap. Over and out.'

A trap? Yes, possibly. Spooks often do try to 'bump me off'. But they never succeed. My lips curl up. No spook is a match for me and HELL'S TALON. Well, except for the evil Grimdorf.

I check the Slayer tools hooked to the belt of my dress. Compass, skull bombs – and my brand new toy, binoculars. But not any old binoculars. This baby can see through walls! This is the gift Swiftfist sent me, the Slayer I never even met. I must remember to thank him at the Slayer's Dinner on Friday night.

So, all set. And, with my scythe clutched in my left hand and my pumpkin lantern clutched in my right, I step warily into the shop.

Even with the help of the gunpowder-enriched candle, it is still awfully dark, a dusty lamp on a desk casting a pathetically dim glow over the books and the musty furnishings. I lift my lantern higher and spot there is a worn-looking sofa sitting under the grimy window. I swallow. It is swathed in cobwebs, the spiders living in them considerably bigger than my balled-up fists.

But, mostly, I just see books. Rows upon rows of them; even piled up in the corners and stacked higgledy-piggledy on the desk. Sadly, most of them seem to be covered in dust, so thick I can make tiny footprints on them with my fingertips.

I creep on, hemmed in by towering bookshelf after towering bookshelf. Cobwebs clutch at my curls and, whenever my foot finds a rug, a puff of dust billows up. It's as if nobody's been in here for months. Nobody with a duster anyway.

'I see you, Slayer.' A sharp, acid-laced whisper

stabs at my mind.

I freeze, the lantern in my fist swaying like a pendulum, dripping wax on my boots.

'Trying to catch me, little girl?'

'No, I...'

'Trying to hurt me?'

I say nothing. Like a lasso, the words drag at my feet, commanding me to turn and flee. But I'm rooted to the floor. It's as if my legs no longer work.

'Soon we will meet. Then, I will hurt YOU.'

'Who – who's there?' I muster, a nervy jitter distorting my words.

The seconds tick ponderously by but there's no answer. But I know who it is. Grimdorf! I don't know how I know, I just do. Gritting my teeth, I command my legs to work and slowly, tiny step by tiny step, I stagger on. My chest is hammering. Thump! Thump! Thump! I just wish I had on a woolly jumper to smoother the echo.

Finally, I'm confronted by a black, panelled door. The wood, I see, is pitted and burnt and the handle is in the rather worrying shape of an upturned claw. Hesitantly, I grasp hold of it and twist. Then, slowly, I push it open.

The next room is even darker; so dark, it looks like a wall and I'll need a hammer to smash my way through. But all I have is my pumpkin lantern. I lift it higher, the gunpowder in the candle crackling and sparking, forcing the inky shadows to draw back. Wax sprays my fingers, burning the tips, but there's no way I'm going to drop it.

NO WAY!

As I skulk down another tunnel of dusty books, I try to step softly, but the 'Tap! Tap! Tap!' of my heels on the wooden floor seems to ricochet off the walls, giving me away. The hand clutching my scythe is trembling, the knuckle waxen and blotched, and my mouth feels as dry as a desert cave.

All of a sudden, just to my left, there is a low growl. I jump, almost dropping my lantern. Is there a dog hiding there? A RABID DOG? No, there can't be. Nobody keeps dogs in Devil's Ash. Too many spooks. Dogs can see them too and they'd be forever barking.

Gently, I rest the lantern on the floor. Then, I stretch up my hand and pull down a book.

On tiptoe, I peek through the gap.

'Oh, sweet Jesus,' I mumble. For there, stooped in a cobwebby corner and swathed in a swirling fog, is the spook of a monster.

A GIGANTIC monster!

Bigger than a bulldozer, it is covered from jaws to claws in a straggly, snowy-white pelt. Jagged teeth the size of elephant tusks erupt from a cave-like mouth and from the top of the skull spring two horns, sharpened to icepicks.

I think..

MY GOD! IT IS! It's the spook of a

YETI!

A gasp of horror slips from my lips. With my knees buckling, I back away, my foot catching the lantern, tipping it over.

THUD! And the candle flickers out.

'Control to Tiffany. Any problems, over?'

I snatch the walky-talky off my belt. 'Oh no,' I rasp into the darkness, my tongue puffed up and dry. 'Everything's hunky-dory. There's just a monster in here who, I think, any second now, will try to murder me.'

A long pause then, 'I think you'll find 'try to murder me, OVER' is the correct way to...'

'GRAMPS!'

Hidden by a wall of books, the yeti snarls menacingly. I hook the walky-talky back on my belt and feel for the lantern. Normally, when I'm in the vicinity of a spook, my blood pumps wildly and I'm much sharper, my night sight perfect. But now I just feel clumsy and blind.

Thankfully, the tips of my fingers swiftly find the pumpkin-shaped light. I twist the top and it flickers back on. Then, urgently, I snatch up my binoculars and put them to my eyes. Amazingly, I can see right through the rows of books to the yeti. He is pacing to and fro, clenching and unclenching his claws. What do I do now, I wonder. My job is to slay the spooks of humans, not the spooks of sixteen foot, furry monsters with claws so big they'd rip a Volvo in half. But no, I'm just being silly. He's not solid; he's only a spook. His claws can't hurt me. So, do I stay and slay him or do I leg it?

But the monster picks for me and, with a spine-chilling howl, he picks up the shelf, showering me with books, and throws it across the shop. A blanket of horror smoothers me. But, but – the yeti's a spook! And no spook, NO SPOOK can pick up solid objects. Well, no spook I know of. TILL NOW!

And now there's nothing standing in his way; nothing between me and a drooling jaw of teeth. A SOLID drooling jaw of teeth!

Slowly, he lumbers over to me.

'Now, let's not be hasty,' I whimper, wishing fervently I knew the Yetish word for 'surrender'. But the monster's not in a prisoner-taking sort of mood and he kicks me so hard in the chest I'm almost knocked to my knees. I toss my lantern at him and swing my scythe at his chest, but the monster's too fast, so fast I can no longer see his claws or feet, but I feel them, in my eye, my jaw, my poor knee.

With a howl, he jumps up, his foot hunting for my chin, but I block it and punch him in the belly. He staggers back, his bushy eyebrows arched. The big wolf, I think, did not expect the tiny lamb to show her teeth.

With fists flying, he clumps back over to me, but I duck, drop low and sweep my foot. Nimbly – for a big, furry monster anyway – he jumps over it. Not good! And now it's his turn.

He thumps me; an uppercut to the jaw. Then he twists and flips me over his shoulder, cartwheeling me to the floor. I clamber drunkenly to my feet but a hammering fist wallops me on the cleft of my chin, cracking my teeth. I lurch back, hitting the bookshop wall and dropping HELL'S TALON. Blurry-eyed, I watch him march up to me, murder glinting in his pot lid-shaped eyes.

'STOP!' I cry. 'This is crazy.' But he is on me like a fat boy on a muffin.

Gripping me by the neck, the yeti slams me back up to the wall. I feel his sharp claws digging into my skin. I grab for his paw, trying to wrench it off, but he's stronger than English mustard.

Suddenly, a rage fills me from my boots to the tops of my curls. I thrust up my chin, the monster's wiry fir scratching the tip of my nose. 'GET – OF – ME!' I wheeze.

The yeti snarls back at me and, in that split second, I see my opening. Yanking a skull bomb off my belt, I twist the top and jam it between two of the monster's jagged teeth.

Instantly, he unclasps my neck and I drop ragdollishly to the floor. Seeing stars, I zigzag over to my fallen scythe and cower there. A split second later,

BOOM!

Very, VERY slowly, I look up.

To my horror, the monster is still on his feet. But, still, I think the bomb injured him. He's swaying back and forth, bulldozing into the wall like a short-circuiting robot. If I'm going to win this fight, now might be my only chance.

In a burst of wild fury, I snatch up my scythe and advance on the yeti. 'Where's Grimdorf?' I yell. 'WHERE?' But the monster is in too much agony to listen.

For a second, I feel terribly sorry for it. I don't want to slay it but I know I must. If I don't, who knows where it will go next; who knows who it will hurt. As Grandad says, it's my duty; it's in my blood. So, with all the venom I can muster, I chop at the foggy swirls, sending the monster howling and yowling back to hell.

My knees crumple and with a pathetic, almost babyish whimper, I fold to the floor. There I stay, my scythe resting on my lap. I can't keep doing this. I just can't. It's killing me...

'Hello? Tiffany? Is everything OK? Over.'

Bow-shouldered, I put the walky-talky to my lips and press the button. 'I slayed it,' I tell him blankly.

'Tiffany! Honestly, you must try to remember to say...'

'Gramps! Just shut up and listen to me. The yeti, it picked up a shelf of books, it threw it at me!'

'So, not a spook then.'

'Yes,' I hiss. 'It was. There was swirling fog and – EVERYTHING!'

For a long, LONG second, all there is is static. Then, in a very husky whisper, Grandad says, 'But a spook can't lift up...'

'IT ALMOST STRANGLED ME!' I howl, cutting him off. 'I FELT THE MONSTER'S CLAW!'

'But – but, that's impossible,' he stutters back. 'Utterly impossible.'

'I KNOW IT IS!' I yell. Inflamed, I toss the walky-talky on the floor. But a spook is just wisps of energy, foggy swirls and goo. So how did it...

Pulling my knees up to my chin, I begin to rock to and fro. This is crazy! I feel as if, any second now, a volcano is going to erupt under my feet or soon a comet is going to hit the planet and I'm standing right where it is going to hit. And all Grandad can do is deny everything.

WHAT IS GOING ON!?

CHAPTER 7

NOT A PRAM-PUSHING MUMMY

STANDING IN THE LUNCH QUEUE, I SCOWL nastily at the dinner lady. She is sooooooo slow! Her only job is to say, 'Chips or salad, luv?' and everybody, EVERYBODY always says, 'Chips.' So, what's the hold up? Here I am, being hunted by a flesh-dripping warlock and I can't even get a bowl of chips to keep my spirits up.

Pardon the pun.

'He's looking at you,' chirrups Izzy, nudging me in the ribs.

'WHO?' I snap, twisting on my heel and scowling at the girl behind me.

But Izzy seems unperturbed by my anger and simply rolls her eyes. 'Troy, y' bozo. Look! Over there under the basketball hoop.'

Ballooning my cheeks, I scan the dinner hall.

'NO!' she whispers urgently. 'Don't look. He'll see you.'

'But you just...' Clenching my hand, I rub my swollen eye with it. I'm so not in the mood for Izzy's matchmaking antics.

Anyway, I don't think anybody is going to be too keen to hold my hand at the moment. I look a total mess. The fight with the yeti left my chin swollen, my front tooth cracked and my left eye just a narrow slit. I had to tell everybody I was in a car crash – WITH A BULLDOZER!

'Wotcha.' A lanky girl with freckly cheeks and bushy curls strolls over and winks playfully at me. 'I see Troy's got his eye on you.'

'How odd,' mutters Izzy flippantly. She's much shorter than me; considerably plumper too, and she always seems to be sucking on the cuff of her jumper as if it's a lolly.

With a roll of my eyes, I turn my back on them and begin to throw glowery daggers at the dinner lady. How can anybody be this slow? She must, I think, be distantly related to a sloth.

'What's up, Stroppy?' Matilda asks.

'I'm ruddy starving,' I growl. This morning, Grandad insisted I forgo my bowl of Sugarpuffs for a bowl of broccoli.

BROCCOLI!

'You need your greens,' he told me with a maddening grin.

'Snot's green,' I mumbled back, staring at the bowl in horror.

Mercifully, he then scuttled off to fetch me a cup of bats milk so I was able to scoop most of it up and drop it into my schoolbag. But now there's mushed-up goo all over my calculator.

'He's so sweet,' murmurs Izzy with a wistful sigh. Suddenly, she tugs on my shirt. 'I forget to tell you. Troy's planning to kiss you at his birthday party. Casper told me.'

I eye her scornfully. 'No, he did not,' I snarl, but I feel my cheeks turn crimson anyway.

Izzy nods feverently, chewing on the cuff of her granny-knitted jumper. 'He did! He did! Honest.'

'Casper in Physics or Casper in German?' Matilda asks, applying strawberry-scented lip gloss.

'German.'

Grinning impishly, Matilda drops the lip gloss in her blazer pocket. 'He's sort of sweet too.'

Suddenly, I feel the eyes of a spook on me. With a scowl, I twist on my heels. There! Over by the door. The chalky-white ghost of a mummy. Sadly, not a pram-pushing sort of mummy, but a grunting, growling sort of mummy. The sort who belongs in a pyramid, not a school canteen. Mercifully, nobody can see him but me and he

SEEMS to be behaving. For the moment, anyway.

I feel myself slowly relax.

Trying to mentally block out the titters of my two annoying pals, I mull over my problems. This morning, over my brimming bowl of broccoli, I attempted to discuss the yeti with Grandad, particularly the monster's amazing ability to throw books and almost throttle me. But, amazingly, Grandad just laughed it off and insisted, 'Odd things happen.'

Odd things happened!' I stormed. 'ODD THINGS HAPPEN!'

But he just told me not to worry and dropped another sprig of broccoli in my bowl.

Then, I brought up Imelda Cartwright. Well, it was as if I'd asked him about the birds and the bees. Instantly, his cheeks went ashen-grey. Then, he rushed from the kitchen insisting he was terribly late for the dentists which, I thought, was distinctly odd as he only has two teeth. So there was no chance for me to even bring up spotting Grimdorf by the snapdragon patch. I sigh. But, perhaps, it was for the best. For all I know, the old codger's got a dodgy ticker.

So many problems but there's nothing I can do. Mentally, I pop them all in a box and shift it to a cobwebby corner in the back of my mind.

'Miss Stern forced me to sit next to Benny Flint in Chemistry,' says Matilda, theatrically pinching her nostrils.

'Yuck!' Izzy pulls a face, her nose wrinkling up like a walnut. 'He reeks. My mum bumped into his mum in ASDA and she's a bit smelly too.'

They both giggle.

'Did you know,' whispers Matilda, sidling up to me and accidentally stepping on my foot, 'Sheryl Bumbly and Alex Ivory snogged.'

'Oooo!' gasps Izzy, sounding a lot like a demented owl.

'Yep.' Matilda nods adamantly. 'On the swings in Lucifer Park.'

'Who told you?' Izzy asks.

'Emily. Her mum's a doctor and Sheryl went to see her. It seems she got a splinter in her bottom from the swing.'

Looking grave, Izzy nods. 'Her bottom is gigantic.'

I see the boy in front of Jessy just piled a ton of chips in his bowl. Greedy pig! I begin to worry how hungry Jessy is and try not to panic.

'Tiffany!' chirrups Izzy, nudging me in the ribs. 'Troy's eyeing you up.'

'No, he's not,' I snap back, trying not to look. 'So stop being so stupid.' But I can't help myself and I glance over. Oh, but he is grinning at me. Forgetting my cracked tooth, I smile coyly back, a tiny ray of sunshine twinkling in my tummy. He is very hunky and he has the most sparkly teeth ever. He should do a TV advert for Colgate. To be honest, he's perfect. He's the only boy I know who smells of peppermint chews.

I decide, then and there, that I will go to Troy's birthday party. Even if I am being hunted by a deranged monster! If only I can think of a way of escaping the dinner Grandad's planned. I know. I'll tell him I feel unwell and pretend to slip off to bed. He will be so busy with the other Slayers, he won't miss me anyway.

Feeling considerably cheered up, I look back to the dinner lady. It's my turn at last.

'Chips,' I peep, trying not to drool on the canteen floor. 'Lots and lots of chips.'

'Sorry, Tiffany.' She shrugs, waving her wooden spoon at the now empty dish. 'Jessy took the last of 'em.'

'But, but...'

'Hold on. OY! HILDA!' she booms, scaring the bejeepers out of me, 'Y' GOT ANY CHIPS BACK THERE!?'

'NO!' booms back the hidden Hilda. 'But there's a ton of salad.'

With a rumbling tummy, I look at her in total and utter horror.

SALAD!

I turn and glower at Jessy Cross who is now

over by the cash register. Yep, the greedy pig took all the chips. MY CHIPS! For a second, I'm tempted to rugby tackle him and nab his food

'He wants to see you.'

I twirl on my heels to find the mummy standing two feet in front of me. Ordering my jelly knees to stop trembling, I try not to panic. A spook must never, EVER suspect a Slayer is frightened of it. Saying that, I think the yeti knew.

'Who?' I spit. 'Grimdorf?'

Rocking gently, the mummy nods. His eyes seem to glow with danger like a starving hyena watching a deer with a broken leg. 'He's up in Lurch Manor,' he says, his words menacingly low.

Well, now I know where he is. And now I know where NOT to go. 'I'm not interested,' I tell the spook. 'And, if I see your boss anywhere in Devil's Ash, I'll slay him. Now, bog off.'

But my tormentor just stands there growling at me. Not so surprising. I don't think the term, 'Bog off' existed in 2,000 B.C.

I feel Izzy's elbow in my ribs. 'Who y' talking to,

Tiffany?' She titters. 'A ghost?'

'Defy him,' the spook rasps, stepping closer, 'and he will hurt you.'

'He'll need a very big army to do that,' I boldly shoot off.

The monster snorts, his laugh harsh and rasping like the sharpening of a knife. 'He HAS a very big army,' he snarls.

Standing eye to chest with the mummy, I clench and unclench my fists. He smells disgusting; not sweet at all. So disgusting, I feel the overpowering urge to flush him down a loo. If only I had my Slayer tools with me. Then I'd do the bandaged-up, poo-wafting scumbag.

With a deep growl, the mummy turns and clomps away, the canteen floor juddering with every stomping step. Feeling horribly unsettled, I watch it go. Spooks hover. They ALWAYS hover! So why is this spook clomping? Except for me, I don't think anybody can see it. But, by the looks of the juddering cutlery, everybody can feel it. I remember the yeti and shudder. If I'm not terribly mistaken, the spooks in Devil's Ash seem to be coming to life!

And, on top of that, Grimdorf now wants to meet me. Why, I wonder. Or is it just a trap? A way of luring me over to Lurch Manor so he can do me in. Well, there's no way I'm going.

NO WAY!

'So, what do y' want?' the dinner lady asks me gruffly.

Dazed, I turn to look at her. 'Em...'

I feel Izzy's elbow in my ribs. 'Go for the salad. You don't want to get Sheryl's big bottom.'

Tossing my tray on the floor, I glower`at the two giggling girls. 'Listen up, you bozos. I'm not interested in the size of Sheryl Bumbly's bottom and nor I am interested in the Flint family and whether they smell or not. Oh, and I don't fancy Troy. But what I do fancy is a bowl of chips. SO – GET – A – GRIP!'

The most horrific hush falls on the dinner hall. Everybody is staring, open-mouthed, as if they all want to take a bite out of me. Even Troy! In fact, his chin is almost to his navel and his cheeks look considerably redder than a London bus. I watch in horror as Sheryl Bumbly runs by me crying.

'MISS SPARROW!' Podgy fingers grip my arm. 'Is there a problem?' It's Mrs McGivern.

Shaking off her hand, I drop to my knees to pick up the dropped tray. 'No,' I mutter, not daring to look up at her. I feel my eyes go blurry and my nose begin to prickle. To my horror, I think I might be going to cry. With a sniffle, I clamber to my feet.

'My God!' Mrs McGivern howls. 'What happened to your face?'

'Car accident,' I tell her evenly, 'with a bulldozer.' Then I turn to the astonished-looking dinner lady and ask her, very politely, if she has any broccoli.

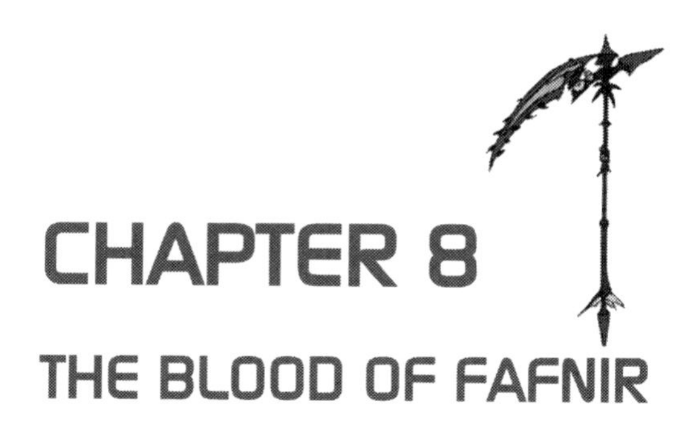

CHAPTER 8

THE BLOOD OF FAFNIR

'ON SEPTEMBER 25th, 1627,' GRANDAD begins his story, 'a baby boy was born in the wee Scottish village of Coffin Creek.'

With a furrowed brow, I plonk my bottom down on the sofa next to him. 'Coffin Creek's not far from here,' I interrupt him. 'Just over the hill.'

With a matching frown, Grandad drums his fingers on his kneecap. 'If you keep butting in,' he scolds me, 'we'll still be sitting here when Swiftfist and the rest of the Slayers show up.'

Oh, yes. I almost forgot. Tomorrow evening is

the BIG dinner. But I'm still planning to slip off to Troy Crook's birthday party. I won't even need to pretend I'm feeling unwell. After a spoonful of the wiggly worm stew Grandad's planning to dish up, I'll probably throw up anyway.

'Sorry, Gramps,' I mutter, flopping back on the sofa and crossing my legs. 'I'll, er – shut up.' I don't want to upset him. Not now he's finally agreed to tell me who Imelda Cartwright is.

'His parents decided to call him Alfred, after his father,' says Grandad, carrying doggedly on, 'and the legend tells he grew up to be a kind, honest boy who enjoyed spending his days with his father, who was the village smithy, helping him to hammer iron to form tools and pots.

'Sadly, when Alfred was only seven, smallpox swept the land and he lost his mother.'

'That's terrible,' I mutter, my eyes welling up. It IS terrible but, to be honest, nowadays I cry for pretty much anything: 'Lost Cat' posters, spilt milk. I remember, I wept for almost a week when the postman stood on Chilli Pepper, my hamster. Poor little thing; he was flatter than a witch's boob.

Grandad's still nattering on so I try not to dwell on my loss. Shoving my hands deeper into the pockets of my dressing gown, I snuggle still deeper into the sofa and focus on the old man's words...

Although terribly saddened by the loss of his beloved wife, Alfred's father was determined to bring his son up properly. So, from then on, it was he who darned the boy's socks, wiped the blood off his cut knees when he fell over and rocked him to sleep when he was sad. The boy, in turn, loved his father very much.

For Alfred's thirteenth birthday, his father forged for him a magnificent scythe. But not from iron, from steel, a newer, much stronger metal. The blade was serrated and razor-sharp and the grip was swathed in dragon skin. When the boy unwrapped it, he jumped for joy. It was the most amazing gift anybody had ever given him.

The next morning, Alfred left his father hammering away in his shed and went with the rest of the villagers to help harvest the crops. But, later that day, when the sun was setting over the hills, Fafnir, a terrifying dragon, attacked Coffin Creek. The boy, on seeing the winged monster hovering over the village, sprinted back. But, by the time he got there, Fafnir had flown away and his father's shed, along with his father, had been burnt to cinders.

In a wild fury, Alfred set off to find the dragon and kill it.

Days turned to weeks, weeks to months and still he hunted. He looked in forests, on the banks of wild rivers, he even travelled to distant lands until, at last, he discovered Fafnir cowering in a cave.

'Why do you keep following me?' the dragon growled when he spotted Alfred creeping into his grotto. 'Wherever I go, wherever I sleep, your shadow hunts me. I grow tired of it.'

'My name is Alfred,' he told the monster. 'My dad's name was Alfred too. Eleven years ago, you attacked a tiny village called Coffin Creek and killed him. Now, I'm here to kill you."

But the dragon, who had grown old and now had rotten teeth and arthritis in his wings, did not want to fight. 'I wish to live,' it whimpered.

'So did my dad,' Alfred hissed back. With a howl of rage. he stormed up to the monster and, using his scythe, slashed open Fafnir's scaly chest.

As the dragon lay dying, Alfred fell to his knees. He felt no better for killing the monster. The hollowness in his stomach he had felt for so long was still there.

Drenched in blood, it suddenly dawned on Alfred why he felt so unhappy. His days were totally and utterly empty. He had no wife to love him, no kids to sit on his knee; there was not even a bronze penny in the pocket of his tatty tunic. In fact, the only thing he possessed was the scythe his father had given to him so many birthdays ago.

Peering down at the blade resting on his lap, Alfred scowled. Fafnir's blood had splattered his cheeks and hands, even the tarnished buttons on his tunic, but the scythe was spotless. It was as if – the blade had absorbed it!

Suddenly, to Alfred's astonishment, the scythe glowed crimson-red. With a cry, he shoved it away and scrambled to his feet. He stood there watching it, hypnotised by the shimmering steel until, after only a few seconds, the metal dulled and turned back to whitish-grey.

Boldly, he stepped up to it and nudged it with his boot. The scythe did not stir. But Alfred wasn't fooled. Not for a second. He knew magic when he saw it. He knew the terrifying power of Fafnir now rested in the cold, pitted blade.

Hastily, he ripped off his tunic and threw it over the scythe. Then he rolled it up. When no metal was showing, he pulled off his belt, hooked it over the curved tip and slung the scythe over his back. Then he set off back to Coffin Creek.

The trip took almost a month, most of it hidden in the cargo holds of ships or in the backs of mule-driven wagons. For the final two days, he travelled on foot, hardly even stopping to drink and sleep till, finally, he got back to his village. There, he went directly to the churchyard, to his father's tomb.

Dropping to his knees, he started to claw at the dirt. With no shovel to help him, his fingers were soon cut and bleeding but, still, he did not stop. Not till the pit he'd dug was six feet long and three feet deep. With aching limbs, he thankfully set the scythe in the ditch and covered it over. Then he rolled over onto his back and fell instantly asleep.

Seven months later, Alfred wed a girl from the village of Devil's Ash. And, ten months after that, they were blessed with the birth of twin boys. For the first time in his adult life, Alfred felt happy. He loved his wife and he adored his kids; but, best of all, the all-consuming lust to kill no longer festered in his chest. He felt free, the spirit of Fafnir forgotten, left to rot in the dirt where it belonged.

Time slipped by and Alfred grew old. His boys ran off to marry and his wife left him for a much richer man. His teeth rotted and the arthritis in his hands hurt him every second of ever day. Like Fafnir, he too lost the will to fight.

His thoughts turned to the object he'd hidden in the dirt. He now regretted killing Fafnir. Yes, the dragon had destroyed much of Coffin Creek and, yes, it had killed his father, but it was a dragon and that's what dragons did. Dogs kill cats, cats kill birds – and dragons, well, they kill men. Soon the power of Fafnir would be lost to the world forever. Alfred knew he had to find a way to stop this from happening. But who to trust the scythe to?

The following night, slumped in the Hangman's Inn, drowning his sorrows, the landlord told Alfred the story of a woman in Devil's Ash who, only a few days ago, had frightened off a terrifying ghost. A warlock called Grimdorf. Pushing away his beer, he listened with growing interest. This woman, he thought, might possess the guts and, most importantly, the wisdom to command the power of Fafnir.

The next morning, he returned to his father's tomb and dug up the scythe. The tunic had almost rotted away so he wrapped it in a blanket. Then, with the oddly-shaped parcel strapped on his back, he set off to find the woman.

Being so old, it took him almost two days to get there. But, when he did, he discovered most of the village had been destroyed. Trees had been uprooted, walls flattened; even the church was now just a jumbled hill of rocks and blackened timbers.

Shocked, he scrambled over the rubble until he stumbled upon a woman binding a bloody cut on a boy's knee. As he drew closer, she looked up and he saw her eyes were even brighter than her long, red curls. This, he knew, was the woman he was looking for.

"How did you stop the ghost?" he asked her blankly. "Magic? Did you put a spell on it?"

'I'm not a witch,' the woman snarled back, 'but there's no way a flesh-dripping skeleton is going to destroy my village.'

'But how did you do it?' Alfred persisted, stepping up to her.

The woman did not flinch or cower away but met his gaze unwaveringly. 'I didn't run away,' she told him simply.

Alfred peered at her thoughtfully. Then, he pulled the lumpy blanket off his back and handed it to her.

'What is it?' she asked, unwrapping it with distrustful eyes.

'If he ever returns, this will help,' he told her. He started to turn away but stopped and, for just a second, the corner of his lips tilted up. 'I was a fool. Mostly. Try to do better.' Then he set off on the long trek back to Coffin Creek.

With a thoughtful frown, I elbow myself up off

the sofa and begin to pace the room. Alfred, when he was a boy, reminds me uncomfortably of me: no Dad, no Mum, just a belly full of hot, bubbling anger. With a shiver, I try to gather my thoughts. 'So, this woman binding the boy's knee,' I say at last. 'She was Imelda Cartwright, was she?'

Grandad chews briskly on his bottom lip. 'Yes, I think so.'

I scowl at him. 'Think?'

'The legend of Alfred is, well – a legend. There's no way of knowing if it's fact or just, well...'

'Gibberish?'

'Indeed.'

'But do you think it's the truth?' I press him.

'Yes.' He nods slowly. 'I do.'

I nod too and carry on pacing. 'And we, er – think she stopped Grimdorf from destroying all of Devil's Ash?'

'Yes, it seems so.'

I stop abruptly and, with a frown, I turn to my grandad. 'Did you say she had red curls?'

'I did.'

'But so do I – and so did Mum.'

'So did your grandmother,' Grandad adds with a grin.

I nod slowly. 'So you were telling the truth. Being a Slayer IS in my blood.'

'Tiffany!' He shoots me a withering look. 'I ALWAYS tell the truth.'

Nobody had ever told me my family had been in the slaying industry for so long. I want to ask Grandad why the big secret, but I stop myself. There's a much, MUCH bigger mystery I must unravel: Why did the spook in my History Class think it so important I discover who Imelda Cartwright was? Unless...

'How did she do it?'

'Sorry?'

'How did Imelda Cartwright stop Grimdorf, the most powerful spook in the world, from destroying the rest of Devil's Ash?'

The old man shrugs. 'It's a mystery. The legend I told you is from a very old book; it is the only record of the event I know of and it only tells, she did not put a spell on him.'

'And she didn't run away,' I add thoughtfully, remembering the words from the story. Folding my knees, I bob down till I'm eye to eye with my grandad. 'This is important,' I say earnestly. 'We must discover how she stopped him.'

But how?' he protests, scratching feverishly at his bristly chin. There's no record anywhere of...'

'Gramps!' I rest a comforting hand on the agitated man's lap. 'When Mum and Grandmother faced Grimdorf, they had HELL'S TALON to protect them and they were killed. When Imelda Cartwright faced him, she only had her wits and she sent him scurrying off in terror. I need to know what she did that they didn't.'

With a nervy swallow, he nods. 'I will do my best, Tiffany.'

'I know,' I say gently. Hopping up, I return to my pacing. Everything is so complicated. I'm often tempted to just run away. Run away till I get to Lands End. I feel my eyes glaze over as I see myself exploring far-off lands. Reluctantly, I turn back to my grandad. 'Why is it you didn't wish to discuss Imelda with me?'

Grandad sits up on the sofa. 'Sorry?'

'This morning, when I asked you who she was, you sprinted off.'

He grunts. 'Not with this leg.'

'Gramps!' I scold him. 'You overtook a speeding bullet.'

He sighs and shrugs. 'I just thought, if you knew the origin of the scythe, it'd put you off using it.'

'Oh!' Now I get it. 'As it's full of blood from a terrifying dragon?'

'Exactly.'

I nod my understanding. I must admit, it is not the most comforting of thoughts. But I still need it to slay spooks. I still need it to slay Grimdorf. But, when Grimdorf's history, I don't think I'll keep hanging over my bed.

I decide to change the subject. 'Gramps, we need to discuss the yeti.'

'OK,' he says warily.

'And how it picked up a shelf of books and lobbed it at me.'

Grandad eyeballs me crossly, puffing out his chest and tucking his thumbs in his pockets. 'A spook can't possibly do such a thing,' he says stubbornly.

'I agree. But the problem is, I saw the yeti do it.'

Just then, there is a sharp knock on the front door and I almost jump out of my skin. 'A Slayer?' I whisper urgently to Grandad.

'It can't be,' he mutters, scratching his brow. 'I'm not expecting them till tomorrow.'

Scowling deeply, I nod. 'Stay here, Gramps,' I order him sternly. Then I creep out of the study and down the corridor to the door. Timidly, I pull it ajar.

Standing there, clutching a bulging folder and a pen, is a woman in a knitted jumper, her specs so big they look like hoops for parrots to sit on.

I feel my body relax. I'm just happy it is not Grimdorf paying another visit to the flower bed. 'Can I help at all?' I ask her cheerfully, pushing open the door.

She peers fleetingly down at the folder in her hand. 'I'm looking for No. 13, Butcher's Street. Is this it?'

'Yes.' I nod and watch her pencil a cross in a box.

'I'm Doctor Stump,' she tells me stonily, 'from St Crispin's Hospital. There's been a report of a child being badly injured in a car crash with a bulldozer.' With a frown, her gaze travels over my swollen chin and cut lips. 'Hmm,' she puts another cross in another box, 'by the look of it, it must be you.'

CHAPTER 9

FOOTSTEPS!

I SLEEP VERY BADLY, ROLLING OVER AND over, cocooning myself in my blankets. In my cluttered mind, I'm back in the tunnel, HELL'S TALON clutched in my hand. It is still wall to wall with hooded spooks but, now, finally, I comprehend the words. 'GRIMDORF!' they chant. 'GRIMDORF!'

Slowly, I creep by them, the skulls under my heels no longer ivory-white but blood-red and sticky. A DEMON'S RED CARPET!

I don't know why, but I know this crowd of

spooks will not hurt me. Indeed, many of them bow when they see my shadow. The rest soon follow, like a rippling pond after a rock is thrown in.

Why do they not attack, I wonder. I am a Slayer, the sworn enemy of all spooks. And where is Grimdorf, the monster they chant so ardently for?

But, for now, they seem happy to bow to me. I feel my chest swell. They bow to Tiffany Sparrow. They bow to the Spook Slayer.

My eyes flutter open and, instantly, I know there's a ghost in here with me. Casting off my blankets, I jump up. I snatch my scythe off the wall and turn to face the room, only to find the boy from school hovering over my bed.

'Stop coming in here,' I hiss, jabbing his chest with the tip of the blade.

Gallingly, Boo is looking at him all limpid-eyed.

I think she thinks he's a box of dog chews; no wonder she didn't bark.

'This is my room,' I say sternly. 'No spooks...'

'...allowed. Yes, yes, I know.' He seems annoyingly cool considering I'm a Spook Slayer and he's a spook. 'But there's a tiny problem.'

'Yes, there is,' I agree angrily, advancing on him. 'The problem is you don't understand the word 'privacy'. And it is not tiny!'

Then he says, 'Grimdorf's here' and my angry words abruptly stop. His name is like the honking horn of a speeding cement truck.

'W-where?' I stutter.

'Here.'

'Where here?'

'In your grandad's study.'

'Why's he...'

'Shush!'

Suddenly, there's a menacing foot-on-wood rasp.

'Third step up,' I say matter of factly. I know every dusty corner of this cottage, including the wooden floors. Then, I frown. Grimdorf's a spook and spooks glide. So why did the step...

'Hurry,' insists the boy. 'We gotta go.'

I nod sharply, dismissing the alarming thought. He's right.

I creep over the mess of blankets on the floor by my bed and over to the door. With a nervy swallow, I pull it open and look out. Thankfully, there's nobody there. The boy, I see, is hovering by my elbow. 'Okay,' I whisper. 'Now!'

Softer than prowling cats, we exit my room. It is dark in the corridor but, over on the landing, there is a soft glow.

Brighter!

Brighter!

Brighter!

'He's coming,' whispers the boy gloomily.

'Thanks, Cpt Clever.' I jump to my feet. 'Time to go.' With Boo and the boy chasing my heels, I dash up the corridor to my grandad's bathroom.

'Er, why in here?' he asks as I very gently shut

the door.

'It is the only room with a lock,' I snootily tell him, twisting it. There's a satisfying 'Click'.

'A lock!' says the spook, his eyebrows arched. 'Er, you do know Grimdorf's a powerful wizard. A lock's not going to stop him. A fortress wall's not going to stop him.'

'But can he pull a rabbit from a hat?' I feebly joke, trying to be all tough but not pulling it off. I so want to be the cool, unruffled Slayer boldly facing the killer warlock but, in truth, I'm almost peeing my pjs.

The spook rolls his eyes, carrying on. 'So, I'd bet my life a plywood door is not going to be much of a problem for him.'

'What life?' I mutter unkindly.

The boy turns away and, instantly, I regret my words. I want to say I'm sorry but I'm a Slayer and Slayers never say sorry to spooks.

With narrow eyes, I glower at the door. Sadly, he's also spot on. The thin wood will not stop Grimdorf. If he suspects where I am, he'll be in here in a second.

A door knob clinks. Grandad's bedroom! Thankfully, tonight is his Bingo night and he's not back yet. My chest is now hammering.

Thump!

Thump!

Thump!

I just wish I had on a woolly jumper and not flimsy cotton pjs to smoother the din.

Suddenly, there is a yell of fury. 'WHERE IS SHE?'

My knees buckling, I back away, my foot catching the leg of a stool, tipping it over.

CRASH!

Then, 'She's in there, Master.' There must be another spook with him – the mummy, I think - his sly words a hammer blow.

'The window,' whispers the boy urgently.

I nod and rush over to it. With springs on my

feet, I hop up on the sill but there I stop. In my panic, I'd totally forgotten there's a thirty foot drop. 'No way!' I cry, hopping back down.

'Jump or fight Grimdorf,' the boy coldly tells me. 'Unless you can think of a better plan.'

With thoughtful eyes, I look over at the bathtub. 'Yes,' I hiss, 'I think I can.' Wondering why Grimdorf's not simply gliding through the door, I dash over to the tub, jam in the plug and twist the taps.

'Interesting turn of events,' mutters the boy, drifting over to watch. 'So, y' planning to drown Grimdorf. Hmm, that'll work. If you wish, I can go and fetch my rubber duck.'

'Shut up!' I spit. Slumping to my knees, I drop HELL'S TALON, clasp my hands together and begin to recite the Lord's prayer.

'Okay,' the boy says slowly. 'This is a bit embarrassing. You know, it's not even Sunday.'

Keeping my eyelids tightly shut, I keep on praying.

'Look, Slayer, I, er – don't wish to interrupt, but

a big, smelly monster's on his way in.'

Gritting my teeth, I twist my neck to look. The boy's right! A bony hand is slowly, jerkily emerging from the wood and Boo, in a wild frenzy of growls and yaps, is snapping at it. 'DRAT!' I snarl. Keeping my fingers crossed a short prayer will do the job, I cup my hands and dunk them into the bath water. 'Get back, Boo!' I yell. Then I scramble to my feet and toss the water at the door.

Like fat in a frying pan, Grimdorf's fingers start to sizzle and spit and, with a cry of agony, he pulls his hand back.

'Holy water,' I smugly inform the boy, snatching up HELL'S TALON. 'Well, sort of.'

'Clever,' he says. But very reluctantly I can tell.

With the boy hovering by my elbow and Boo still growling menacingly, I warily eye the door. What, I wonder with a gulp, will the evil spook try next.

The seconds tick slowly by. An owl hoots in the conker tree by the window. The taps drip. But there's no sign of the evil spook.

'Do you think he's still there?' I finally murmur.

'I don't know,' whispers back the boy. 'Stay here. I'll try to...'

'Slayer.' A snarl laced with fury. 'I need it. I need it NOW! Hand it over and I will be – merciful.'

I frown and shoot the boy a quizzical look. He shrugs back at me. His eyes look wild; darting here, there and everywhere. I think he's enjoying himself!

'HAND IT OVER!' Grimdorf's cry ricochets off the walls, pummeling my body and making the door judder.

'BARK!' barks Boo. 'BARK! BARK! BARK!'

KAPOW!

A bomb seems to blow up in my skull...

CUTTING

SPLICING

RIPPING AT MY MIND!

With a yell of agony, I drop my scythe, clawing at my eyelids. 'Stop this!' I cry. 'STOP!'

'Whatever you say,' he jeers.

Instantly, the throbbing lessens as if I just swallowed the world's most powerful Aspirin. Slowly, I lower my hands. My jaw drops to my chin and my knees turn to jelly. To my utter astonishment, I'm on a ship. And, I think...

OH NO! IT IS...

The ship's sinking!

CHAPTER 10

HENRY'S TINY FINGERS

A UNIFORMED MAN IN A PUFFED-UP yellow vest elbows by me, knocking me to the deck. For a split second, he falters, then terror balloons in his eyes and he sprints off. 'Sorry, Miss,' he calls belatedly over his shoulder.

I clamber to my feet. 'Moron,' I mutter, nursing a scratch on my hand.

I see I'm no longer in my cotton pjs. Now, I'm dressed in a long, flowery gown and, under it – I peek – FRILLY BLOOMERS! A bonnet crowns my curls and flimsy slippers cover my feet. I prod my top lip with my tongue and taste lipstick.

The tilting deck is slowly flooding, the water swirling over my slippers. Gingerly, I drag my feet up the ship and away from the rising water. A tall, white funnel looms over me, lit up by the moon and, in a corner, a tiny orchestra of violins and a forlorn-looking cellist play a cheerful melody.

Most of the passengers milling the deck look dazed; I know that look. I remember seeing it in the mirror the day my mum was killed. They think the alarm clock will soon ring and they will sit up in bed and stretch. They need to be told what to do but nobody, it seems, wants the job.

Peering over a metal banister, I discover I'm on a colossal ship and almost half of it is under water. A rocket zooms up into the night sky, exposing a lifeboat full of weeping children and silent mums. Wheels crank and men grunt as it is lowered down to the glassy water.

'Put this on, lass,' another uniformed man stuffs a vest in my hands, 'and get to safety.'

Instantly, I grip the hem of his jacket. 'What ship

is this?' I bark. 'Where am I?'

But he's in too much of a hurry. Pulling free, he jogs off, flinging vests to the rest of the frightened passengers.

Wrestling to put it on, I spot a word embossed on the front and I get the biggest shock of my life. I suddenly find it very difficult to focus my eyes. I drop to my knees, the word embedded in my mind.

TITANIC!

Did Grimdorf send me here? But – why? And how did he do it? Is his magic so powerful? Suddenly, all my other problems seem unimportant. Even Dr Stump insisting I visit St. Crispin's Hospital every two weeks for a check up.

I feel myself slipping, The ship is slowly keeling over, whimpering in her agony. Urgently, I jump to my feet and grip hold of the banister. I must keep dry for as long as I can. If this IS the

Titanic then, I remember from History Class, the water is icy cold.

Further up the deck and, thankfully, away from the rising water, I spot a portly man in a top hat and with curly whiskers. Hand over hand. I struggle over to him. 'I need help,' I pant. 'I must get off this ship.'

The man chews off the tip of a cigar and spits it out. 'Cuban,' he informs me, patting his pockets. 'Cost me twenty shillings. Can I possibly bother you for a light?'

'Em, no. Sorry.' I scowl at him. 'You do know this ship is sinking?'

'Yes, my girl, I do. Anyway, I'm Lord Cavendish-Brown.' He bows stiffly. 'You know, I do enjoy a good cigar but, it seems, I left my lighter in the cabin. Awfully annoying. I must send my man to fetch it. Now, where is the fellow? He's always slacking.'

I look at him in bewilderment. He's bonkers!

Pulling off my vest, I stuff it in the man's hands. 'Put it on,' I order him. 'I think it knots at the front.'

Then, throwing off the silly bonnet and slippers, I stumble away.

I must find a way off this doomed ship. But how? Where do I go? I rub my hands briskly together. It's so cold and, here I am, dressed for a July night in the Sahara Desert.

The high-pitched screech of twisting metal rings in my skull and I look up to the see the funnel slowly toppling over. 'LOOK OUT!' I howl to a bonneted lady up to her knees in swirling water. A split second later, the hunk of metal lands in the water with a splash, crushing her.

Unblinking, I look on in horror, my feet rooted to the deck of the ship.

Over to my left, there is a yelling crowd of passengers who seem to be trying to get off the Titanic too. But a tall man in a uniform, holding a pistol, is keeping them back. 'Children first,' he hollers.

Excellent, I think. I'm 'children'.

Sprinting over, I begin to jostle my way through the angry mob. A lady in a red ball gown steps on my foot and a chunky man with a monocle elbows me in the eye. But I keep on going, pushing and shoving, forcing my way to the front.

At last, I get there, but the last of the lifeboats is already being lowered.

'But there's still room,' I holler indignantly at the man.

With a hardening jaw, he says nothing.

'Listen to me!' I screech, snatching at his sleeve.

Like lightening, he lowers the pistol till the tip of the barrel is tickling the tip of my nose. 'Step away,' he commands me, his words shaking almost as much as the gun in his hand.

'Okay! Okay!' I whimper, hastily backpedalling and wishing I'd not left HELL'S TALON in my Grandad's bathroom.

The angry spark in his eye flickers out and, with a look of disgust, he casts the pistol away. 'Sorry,' he murmurs. 'Try over on the port side. You might be lucky.'

I nod. 'Thanks,' I say, turning away.

'But hurry,' he tells me, his hand pressing urgently into my back.

I trip and stumble my way over the slippery wood. Steeper and steeper, the Titanic tilts over so I must grip hold of iron ladders and the corners of doors to prevent myself from hurtling off the ship. Everywhere, men helter-skelter over the lopsided deck, yelping in panic and crying for help.

Scrambling over a fallen mast, I finally get to the port side of the ship. But, to my horror, all I find there is a metal winch and a dangling rope.

Urgently, I turn to a bedraggled crowd of passengers clinging to the winch. 'Where did all the lifeboats go?' I yell.

They ignore me but for a scruffily-dressed woman who is perched on the top of the banister. 'They left us,' she whimpers, looking at me beseechingly. 'The posh lot left us here to drown.' She pulls her legs up and over the top bar.

'No!' I holler, running towards her. But I'm too late and she jumps, her cry filling the bitterly cold night.

A deep, low growl erupts in the belly of the ship and the lights blink off. I stand there, just – stand there, only a tiny whimper invading my terror. The twinkling stars help me to spot a tiny boy; he is sitting, his knees up to his chin, under a ladder. I rush over and kneel down next to him.

'Where's your mummy?' I softly ask him. I see that his hand is shaking. On impulse, I cover it in my own.

'I lost her,' he snivels, his words trembling. He has on stripy pjs and boots on his feet; he looks to be seven or so. 'Can you help me to find her?'

I nod, squeezing his hand. 'Soon,' I promise him. 'If I can.'

The ship is almost vertical now, only the ladder welded to the wall preventing the boy and I from sliding away. Soon, I know, the rest of the ship will be under water and we will be thrown to the mercy of the freezing Atlantic.

Only seconds to go.

I remember the boy wedged in next to me. 'I'm Tiffany,' I tell him.

'H-H-Henry,' he stutters back.

'So,' I frown, trying to think of things to say; difficult to do when sitting on the sinking Titanic, 'what do you do for fun? Play football? Watch TV?'

'What's a TV?' the boy asks.

'Oh, yes. Sorry.' I muster a grin; I forgot it's 1912 and TV's not been invented yet. 'Don't worry, when you get to sixty...' I stop, the rest of my words jammed in my larynx. Any second now, Henry's going to drown. No TV for him...

Then...

The swirling water hits me, surging up and over my body and filling my nostrils. It is agony, like hundreds and hundreds of tiny pins jabbing at my skin. Grimly, I hold onto Henry's hand and I feel his tiny fingers squeezing me back.

He must be so frightened. But there's nothing I can do to help him and, for the first time in my life, I feel totally and utterly powerless.

As I slowly drown in the icy waters of the Atlantic, a terrific fury suddenly erupts up within me. Fury at Grimdorf; that he will now destroy Devil's Ash and there's nobody to stop him. Fury at Grandad for being so shifty and difficult and not properly helping me. But, most of all, fury at Mum and Dad; if only they'd...

All of a sudden, I feel my body being yanked upwards as if I'm hooked on a fishing line, and I feel the boy's tiny fingers slipping from my grasp. A split second later, oxygen fills my bursting lungs and a velvety warmth smothers my skin.

Slowly, I lift my eyelids, half expecting to be sitting on a fluffy cloud, tiny angel wings fluttering on my back. But, to my jaw-dropping astonishment, I SEEM to be standing in a big, green tent!

'Well, this is much better,' I mutter.

CHAPTER 11

BULLY TINS AND BARBED WIRE

'RELAX TROOPER. GRAB A PEW. DROP of rum? NO? Good boy. You troopers drink too much anyway. Wonderful news! We go over the top at dawn.' The curly-moustached man sitting on the stool in front of me titters. 'When I say 'we', not me. You! You and your men. Lucky blighters! I must stay here; plan the next skirmish. I volunteered you by the way. Your regiment gets to fly the flag for England.' He flaps a hand at me. 'No, no, don't thank me. Now, have a butchers at this map. The Hun's here, dug in on the hill; they been up there for months. The only way to get to them is a full on attack. Sappers been tunnelling for months. They plan to stick a bomb under the German trench and blow it up. Then, over you go. Willy Biggins will be on your flank. Excellent fellow. I play cricket with his dad. Well, I did. He lost his leg to a cannon ball. We plan to shell the blighters good and proper too. They'll be in shock by the time you get to them. They'll probably surrender or run off. A stroll in the park for your lads.'

I look blankly at him. Is he talking to me?

I'm standing in a green, canvas tent. The old fellow sitting at the desk in front of me is in a uniform and so, it seems, am I. My feet feel cramped in tall, black boots and my skin is itchy under my woolly tunic. I'm still pretty cold but thankfully not as cold as when I was drowning in the freezing Atlantic. I have on a metal helmet and a rifle is slung over my shoulder.

I flex my fingers. Only a second ago I'd been holding Henry's tiny hand. Poor kid. I hope he survived.

'Chat to your men, check gasmasks and bayonets. Bacon and jam for every fellow when they get back; and a day's rest too. Keep low and watch for snipers. How's the trench foot?'

'Em...'

'That bad, is it? Try a drop of whale oil. That'll do the trick. Ok, that's all, Trooper. Chop! Chop! Remember, if successful, the Battle of the Somme will end the war.'

I look to my feet, wondering what trench foot is. He keeps calling me Trooper but can he not see I'm a teenage girl? I'm not even in the scouts.

He throws me a salute and I sort of wave feebly back.

Stumbling from the tent, I'm met by a gangly man caked collar to boots in mud. 'What did he say, Sir? We going over?'

'Yes,' I reply. 'I, er – think so. I lift off my helmet. 'At dawn.'

The man's shoulders droop. 'Then we'd better get back and tell the lads the good news.'

I nod.

Hunched over, he sets off. 'Sir,' he calls, not bothering to look back, 'better pop your tin potty on. Lots of snipers.'

Shoving my helmet back on, I reluctantly follow him.

The night is pitch black, the moon having run away in disgust; and it is snowing in big, fat lumps. There is a sudden flash of light followed by a boom and, suddenly, the sky is lit up for a second showing me a barren wilderness of muddy hills and burnt trees. A pony staggers by dragging a wagon. To my horror, I see it is jammed full of injured men crying and whimpering.

I'm in a world of rattling guns, whiz-bangs and barbed wire.

Trudging on, I keep my hands hidden in my deep pockets. Hanging over my shoulder, the rifle keeps nudging me, reminding me of where

Grimdorf has sent me.

To war!

'Is that you, Spink?'

'No, it's bleedin' Santa. Lower y rifle, dimwit.' Following Spink, I clamber down into a deep trench. 'Open y' lugs, lads,' Spink yells. 'Sir here, has a wonderful job for us.'

There must be fifty men in the trench. Swimming in mud, they sit there scoffing lumps of grisly-looking beef from battered tin trays; bully tins if I remember correctly.

Forks clatter to a stop and they all look at me expectantly.

'Is it true, Sir?' a young-looking trooper pips up, his eyes scared and bloodshot.

I look at him. How old? Sixteen? Seventeen? A few years older than me. 'Yes,' I reluctantly say. 'At dawn. After we shell them and the Sappers blow up the German trench.'

'The General says it'll be a 'stroll in the park',' offers up Spink. He must have been listening at the tent flap.

My lips suddenly feel terribly dry. I remember studying the Battle of the Somme in History. It had been a bloodbath. But I nod anyway.

Many of the men grin but I spot Spink looks much less cheerful at the prospect of attacking the Germans. I suspect he knows the terrible truth too.

Spink elbows the man sitting next to him. 'What did y' get?'

'Sweets,' he pops a yellow blob in his mouth, 'and a letter from my dad.' He looks up at me. 'Can you tell me what it says, Sir? Never been much good with words. A bit fiddly, I find.'

I nod. Moving over to stand next to a lantern, I unfold the damp paper.

Hello Jacob my boy,

Your mum and I hope this letter finds you well and in good spirits. She sends her love and told me to tell you she prays for you and your regiment every Sunday in church. Every day, the newspapers tell how gallantly the British army is fighting. It seems the Germans will surrender any day now and the war will finally be over.

The men in the trench guffaw at this.

'If only they knew,' mutters Jacob dejectedly.

Yesterday, I chatted to Mr Crunch, your old boss over at the wood mill. He told me there's plenty of work so, when you return, there's a job for you. Oh, and the roof on the chicken hut needs fixing too but I will hold off doing it until you can help me.

Now for the bad news. Your old football chum, Billy Potts, got hit in the eyes by shrapnel. Sadly, he's blind now but back with his family. I met his dad in the pub and he told me his son's not doing too well. When you get back you must visit him and try to cheer him up.

Cathy is dating a doctor from St Crispin's Hospital. She's very keen and we hardly ever seem to see her. Oh, and Granny's dog got shot by a farmer.

Enjoy the lemon bonbons and, by the way, your mum is knitting socks for you. Will send shortly.

Thinking of you,

Dad

'Who's Cathy?' I ask, gently folding up the letter and passing it back to him.

'My sister.' Jacob slips it into his tunic pocket. 'Poor Billy, good lad, played keeper for The King's Arms.' He grins. 'Let in so many balls we all thought he was blind anyway.' He turns to Spink. 'What did you get?'

'A letter from my mum,' says Spink, wiping down his bayonet with a rag, 'and my granny. My sister too. I think even the dog put paw to paper. But nobody sent me socks. My left foot's killing me.'

Trench foot. I remember Mum always told me to keep my feet dry and warm. I remember what the General in the tent told me too. 'Try whale oil,' I suggest.

Spink nods. 'I will. Cheers, Sir.'

'Y' not opening y' letters?' Jacob says to him.

'No.' He shrugs. 'When I get back.'

'But what if...'

Spink lobs a bully tin at him. 'If I'm killed, Granny's bad knees and my sister Sally's antics in the hayloft will be of no interest to me. But if I'm not, I can enjoy all the gossip over a bacon roll and a pot of jam.'

I perch on a rusty petrol drum and idly listen to the chatter of the men. Why did Grimdorf send me here? To France? To a muddy trench in World War One. Reluctantly, I look at my watch. Not long now. It's been a long night, sitting here, checking off the hours till dawn. Mostly, the men let me be, content to sit and chat: food and the lack of it, woman and the lack of them. A Welsh fellow attempted to sing 'Oh, Danny Boy' but the British guns were making such a racket drumming the

German trench, he'd given up. During the night, the General had dropped by to tell the men what a very important job they were going to do. It seems I'm a sort of officer too. The men call me 'Sir' and look to me for support so I try to look confident and say, 'Chin up' and 'Soon be over' every opportunity I get.

A thundering boom rocks the trench. Staggering, I fall to my knees, mud drenching my body. Spink helps me up.

'This is it,' he cheerfully tells me. 'The Sappers just blew up the German trench.'

In a daze, I nod. Panic is starting to creep over my body. I'm finding it difficult to swallow and my lips feel puffed up and dry. The men gather by the foot of the ladders. I stumble over to them. There's no words left in me but for a husky, 'Good luck' to the man praying by my elbow.

If Grimdorf's watching, I hope he plans to whisk me away if a bullet has Tiffany Sparrow etched on it.

'Y-you too, Sir.' A stuttered reply, dripping with

terror.

Hugging.

Handshaking.

Then, a whistle blows.

A grim-looking trooper clambers up the ladder. Clutching a rifle I don't know how to work, I clamber up after him.

Peering over the top, a labyrinth of muddy craters meet my eyes. I feel my knees almost buckle as mortars spit and guns clatter, 'YAK! YAK! YAK!'

A man below me on the ladder slaps my foot. 'Get going, Sir!'

Scrambling up the last two rungs of the ladder, I set off, but my boots trip over a body slumped in the mud and I tumble to my knees. It is Jacob, his eyes glassy and staring.

A hand grabs me by the belt and yanks me to my feet. 'Keep up,' says Spink. 'Bacon and jam when we get back.'

I nod, not comprehending a word.

We rush on, clattering guns spraying a lethal

storm of metal at us. Everywhere, men fall in the mud. Spink falls too and I drop to my knees next to him.

Trembling, his tunic torn and bloody, he grabs for my hand. 'I wish I'd opened my letters,' he sputters. 'God, I miss my mum.'

I nod. 'Me too.'

'And my foot's still murdering me.' He titters, spilling blood on his chin.

Gritting my teeth, I clasp his fingers tightly. 'I'm going get you the warmest woollen socks I can find,' I tell him. 'The very best.'

I feel a hammer blow to my stomach and I keel over, my body covering Spink.

Over my limp form, the guns keep clattering away. They seem not to worry that all the troops have been killed.

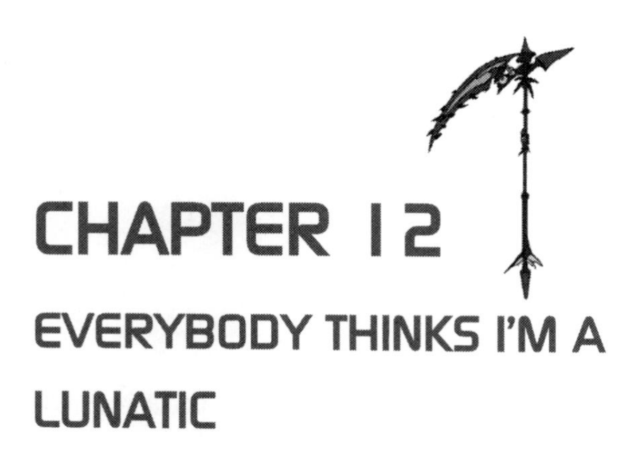

CHAPTER 12

EVERYBODY THINKS I'M A LUNATIC

'TIFFANY!' I JUMP UP, KNOCKING MY elbow on the corner of a filing cabinet. 'Pop over to Sally's office, will you?' A chubby man hands me a sheet of paper. 'Oh, and tell her the meeting is now at ten thirty and not eleven.' He scowls at me. 'Chop! Chop! Soon be lunch.' Then he twists on his heels and lumbers off.

Nodding dumbly, I gently pat my stomach.

Then I peek down the front of my shirt. No blood; not even a tiny scar.

Looking up, I see I'm now in a modern-looking office. Everywhere, fingers tap plastic keys and coffee mugs sit on cluttered desks. A skinny man is photocopying and a flashing fax beeps and spills paper on the grey carpet.

I stand and listen for a second. From the accents, I think I must be in America.

I feel the knot in my stomach slowly unwind. Compared to being on the sinking Titanic or in a muddy trench, fighting Germans, this is much, MUCH safer. Unless a rogue stapler or a pencil sharper suddenly attacks me.

Now, what to do with this silly memo? I wander over to the lifts. Perhaps Sally's office is on a different floor.

So, up or down?

Up.

I press the button. A gold arrow over the doors twirls...

94, 95, 96

Wow! This tower is tall. It must be a skyscraper. The doors slither open with a 'PING!' but I don't step in. The most terrifying thought just hit me.

No.

No way!

No way Grimdorf sent me there.

Dropping Sally's memo on the carpet, I dash over to the photocopy man. 'What day is it?' I bark at him.

He turns to look at me. Then he rubs his bristly chin. 'The 12th, I think.'

Thank God!

'No, no. Hold on.' He wags a finger at me. 'I took the bus up to Boston yesterday to see my old pops. It was his birthday. He turned 87 on the 10th, so today must be...'

My jaw sags. 'The 11th,' I mutter.

The man nods. 'Yep. The 11th of September.'

Oh no! I feel a shiver run up my spine, OH NO! I

sprint over to the window and there, rising up from the city of New York, is a second silver tower. Grimdorf's sent me back to 2001, to the twin towers. And, any moment now, terrorists will fly jumbo jets into them, killing everybody.

I scan the sky but there's nothing to see. I look over at a clock on the wall.

8.37

No help there. I can't even remember if it happened in the morning or the afternoon. Anyway, it's not important. My job now is to get everybody out. Including me!

'Tiffany, did you find Sally and tell her?'

I twist on my heels to find the chubby man looking crossly at me.

'W-what?' I stammer.

'I told you to...'

'We must go.'

'No,' the man says slowly. 'YOU must go to

Sally's...'

'WE MUST GO!' I snarl savagely.

With a frown, the man steps back. 'Tiffany, I know it's a little hot in here but...'

Sprinting over to a desk, I jump up on it, knocking over a pot of pens, scattering them on the carpet. 'Listen to me,' I yell. 'Any second now, a passenger jet is going to hit this tower.'

A stony hush meets my words. Everybody in the room turns to look at me. Then, as if they all telepathically agreed I'm a total and utter lunatic, they go back to work.

'Get down off the desk, Tiffany.' It is the photocopy man. 'I rang Security.'

But, over the top of his shiny skull, I just spotted a 'BLOB' moving in the sky. A bird?

A VERY, VERY BIG BIRD?

Jumping down, I elbow by the man and run over to the window. 'Tiffany,' he begs, scampering after me. 'This is crazy.' Ignoring him, I press my nose up to the glass.

'My God,' I murmur. Twisting on my heels, I grip

the man's jumper. 'There it is,' I tell him. 'THERE IT IS!'

'Having a spot of bother, Tony?' A woman in a red cap walks over. Security!

Tony shrugs. 'Tiffany here's acting a bit - odd.'

'No, I'm not!' I seethe, I wave an emphatic hand at the window. 'Look! You see there. The plane. Well, any second now, it's going to hit this tower. We must get everybody out of here. We must,' I chew vehemently on my lower lip, trying to think, 'I know! Set off the fire alarm.'

The woman frowns at me. Then she lifts her chin and sniffs. 'I can't smell any smoke,' she says.

This is getting me nowhere. With a growl, I rush back over to the lifts. I remember seeing...

Yes! There! By the silvery doors, a red box on the wall.

In the Event of Fire

Smash the Glass

I lift my fist but a hand grabs it, pulling me away.

'Get off me!' I cry.

'Now, now, try to relax...'

'Er, Lucy,' Tony prods the woman in the ribs, 'that jet is flying very low.'

I feel her hand loosen. Twisting to look too, I feel my knees turn to jelly.

TIME'S UP!

'Grab my hand.' Amazingly, the boy spook from History Class is standing by my elbow. Not hovering! STANDING! 'NOW!' he bawls.

'But, but – I gotta try to help them.'

'You can't.'

'Why?'

'Even a Slayer can't alter history.'

I swallow and, with a jerky nod, I put my hand in his. Amazingly, I feel his fingers gripping me.

Then, suddenly, the floor shivers under my feet and the screech of twisting metal rings in my skull. For a split second, I feel the skin on my cheeks melt and my eyebrows burn. Then, a frosty wind blows over me and, slowly, I drag open my eyes.

I'm back in the bathroom – and my cotton pjs – the boy, my rescuer, no longer standing, but hovering by my elbow. Instantly, my hand falls through his. He's back to being a spook. My enemy.

A pitiless whisper drills into my mind. 'Enjoy the history lesson?' Grimdorf scoffs me.

'But – WHY?' I snarl.

'Ships sink, men kill men, terrorists hijack passenger jets. Nobody can stop it happening so why bother to try.'

'I don't understand.'

'My destiny, Slayer, is written in the stars. You will not stop me, you CANNOT stop me, so – why – bother – to – try!'

'You think so, do you?' I hiss back at my hidden tormentor.

'I know so.'

I begin to rock on my heels, my eyelids fluttering. I can feel the anger welling up in me, flooding me belly like hot, bubbling acid. He put me through all of this just to show me how powerful he is and how helpless I am? I clench and unclench my fists. I can still feel Henry's tiny fingers in my hand. I can still smell Spink's blood. With a wild cry, I march over to the door and kick it open. 'If y' wanna fight,' I yell, 'let's fight!'

But the corridor's totally deserted; Grimdorf's nowhere to be seen. I turn to look back at the boy but, now, he's missing too.

Then it hits me.

Where the devil is HELL'S TALON!?

CHAPTER 13

WIGGLY WORM STEW

A TUBBY MAN WITH A CREW CUT AND red, welty skin thumps me so hard on the back, I spill my glass of milk. 'So, how's things?' he bellows. 'Enjoying the exciting life of a Slayer?'

'Oh, er – yes, yes. Mostly. No spook's got the better of me yet.' Then, lifting my chin, I add, 'I slayed a yeti yesterday.'

'A yeti!' Jub Jub's owlish eyes, tinted yellow, gaze doubtfully on my sparkly, pink dress. I feel like a horse being looked over in a paddock and

I wonder if he will ask to see my teeth.

It is Friday night; the night of the Slayers' Dinner and everybody is sitting in the kitchen. I'm elbow to elbow with Grandad and Jub Jub; and, facing me, is Cody Blitz, a dumpy-looking fellow with bushy eyebrows and crimson-red cheeks. He reminds me of a circus clown but without the flippery feet.

Sprawled on the stool next to Cody is Jagger Steel. He is lollipop-skinny, three wispy curls clinging stubbornly to his well-polished skull. Dressed in a scarlet silk tunic and a lumpy pelican-pink cravat, he's a big fan of Grandad's whisky and seems determined to try and drown in it.

Finally, at the far end of the kitchen, by the sink, sits Swiftfist Brent. I eye him for a moment, noting his gigantic shoulders, bulldog jaw and long, spindly fingers; they look all wrinkly as if he pickled them in brine. He's not spoken to me yet – well, not directly anyway, but, every now and then, I feel his eyes flickering my way.

The old Slayer swivels on his stool. 'So, what's in the pot?' he asks Grandad who, right away, hops to his feet and limps over to the oven. 'If I remember correctly, Cody Blitz here served pickled python at the last Slayers' Dinner.' He licks his lips. 'Wonderful stuff. I was farting for weeks.'

Looking frighteningly happy, Grandad lugs the pot over. 'I think I can do even better,' he tells them grandly.

Oh God!

'From deep in the Amazon forest, I bring you WIGGLY WORM STEW!' And, with a showman's 'TA! TA!', he whips of the lid.

With chins in hands, everybody peers keenly in. I look too. There, swimming in a muddy-brown, lumpy-looking, softly-plopping stew is a throng of tiny, wriggling worms.

Speechless, everybody looks at them.

'SURPRISE!' says Grandad.

'Top marks there,' Jub Jub mutters grimly back.

'If only – hic! - Polly and Beryl were here to

enjoy this, er – hic! – food,' slurs Jagger.

'Here's to Polly and Beryl,' hollers Cody, lifting his goblet. I suspect he's just trying to put off sampling the food. Clever man.

'Polly and Beryl,' they chorus.

'Beryl was a wily old bird,' remarks Swiftfist slurping on his beer. 'I was surprised she and Tiffany's mum risked fighting Grimdorf in Lurch Manor where he's strongest.'

Suddenly, it is very silent in the room; except for Jagger who keeps hiccupping.

Grandad rubs frantically at his woolly hat. 'Yes, well – er, I don't know why they went up there,' he stutters, almost running back to his stool. 'Very silly of them. I told them not to.' He drags a snotty-looking hanky from his sleeve and tenderly dabs his reddened nostrils. 'Bit of a cold,' he snivels.

'Indeed.' The old Slayer skewers Grandad with a terrifying scowl, his eyes narrow, wrinkling up his crow's feet.

'Tiffany Sparrow!' hollers Jagger, clambering to his feet, swaying a little and plonking back down.

'SPEECH!'

A scowl knots my eyebrows. 'Sorry?' I mutter. I press my bottom to the top of the stool hoping to weld it there.

'Now, now, don't be shy,' he slurs, wagging a jewel-encrusted finger at me. 'The hosting Slayer's job is to keep his...'

'Or her,' butts in Cody.

With a growl, Jagger throws a fork at him, skewering the other Slayer's cheek.

Chuckling, Cody yanks it out. 'Good shot," he commends him, wiping away the trickling blood.

'Now, where did I get to?' Jagger downs a shot of Grandad's whisky to help him to remember. 'Oh, yes. The hosting Slayer's job is to keep his,' he bows to Cody, 'or her visitors amused with a funny speech. Did y' sly old grandad not tell you?'

'No,' I hiss. 'He did not.'

'Sorry,' mutters Grandad, sinking so far down on his stool, he almost slips under the table. 'It slipped my mind.'

'SPEECH! SPEECH! SPEECH!' they all chant, Jub Jub thumping me playfully on the shoulder and almost dislocating it.

With dry lips, I swallow deeply and stand up. What to say? What to say? All day, the only thing on my mind has been poor Spink and how I'd told him I get him new socks. 'Thanks for coming,' I begin, 'and, er...' Then, it hits me! I need help slaying Grimdorf and, here I am, in a room full of Slayers.

1 + 1 = 2

But how to tell them the shocking news? I decide to go for the 'bull in the china shop' method; it's the best. 'Grimdorf's back,' I tell them bluntly.

'NO, HE'S NOT!' yelps Grandad, hopping to his slippered feet and spilling beer on his jumper.

'Yes, he is,' I say firmly. Stiffening my knees, I glare mulishly at him.

'Tiffany, this is not the...'

'How do you know?' Swiftfist interrupts him.

Looking very put out, Grandad drops back down onto his stool. 'No respect,' he murmurs.

Ignoring him, I timidly turn to the Slayer, his eyes burning the backs of my pupils. 'A spook told me,' I blurt out.'

The seconds tick ponderously by and nobody says a word. Slayers, I know, don't trust spooks.

'And I think he's up in Lurch Manor,' I add.

Looking thoroughly fed up, Jagger tips up the now empty whisky bottle. 'Well, that wasn't a very funny speech,' he remarks.

Jub Jub grunts sceptically. 'But Beryl and Polly slayed him.'

I nod slowly. 'I know. But the thing is, I think, possibly, they didn't.'

'Is this the truth?' Swiftfist growls at Grandad, his chin set firm like granite.

The old man sits up on his stool, seemingly a little surprised to be asked. 'Well, I – er, don't know. According to Tiffany, there's been a lot of odd things happening.'

According to Tiffany! ACCORDING TO TIFFANY! I glare down at his woolly hat. He's my grandad and he can't even back me up.

Cody Blitz slams his fist in his hand. 'Then we storm over to this – Lurch Manor wherever it is and, if he's there, we slay him.'

'Don't be foolish,' growls Swiftfist. 'Remember what happened to poor Polly and Beryl. No, if Tiffany's correct and Grimdorf's back then we mustn't fight him on his territory. He's much too powerful there.'

'Then where?' demands Cody, looking a little annoyed.

The old Slayer frowns and turns to me. 'This Lurch Manor of his is by the cemetery on the top of Ebony Hill, yes? At the end of Bucket O' Blood Lane?'

'Yes,' I reply, my fingers crossed he's going to help me.

'Then Bucket O' Blood Lane is where we'll set the trap. When he exits the manor, we'll ambush him and slay him good and proper.'

With a sigh, I sip my milk. Wonderful! Now I don't have to do it.

'You can show the Slayers the way, Tiffany,' remarks Grandad, spooning stew into a bowl.

'Excellent!' agrees Jub Jub, thumping me even harder on the back.

Choking on my drink, I shakily nod. 'Oh, er – yes, yes. I'd be delighted too. But I think Swiftfist knows the way.'

'TIFFANY!' Jub Jub looks at me reprovingly. 'Remember, this monster murdered your mother and grandmother. This is your chance for revenge.'

I nod soberly. He's right. 'I'll be there,' I tell him. But I don't know how much help I'll be. Not now Grimdorf's stolen my scythe. Oh well, I'll just borrow Grandad's grass clippers from the shed. 'When do we go?' I ask Swiftfist. 'Now?'

The Slayer snorts. 'And miss this succulent dinner? Oh no! We'll set up camp midnight tomorrow.' He thumps the hilt of the sword on his belt. 'And if Grimdorf shows up, I will – well, let's just say, he'll be wetting his knickers and crying for his mummy.'

Cheering, the Slayers clank goblets. 'Wetting knickers!' they holler. Then, embarrassingly, they begin to sing,

We'll hunt 'em in the moonlight
We'll hunt 'em dusk to dawn
Blubbering spooks in moldy boots
Trembling till we yawn

'Gramps,' I whisper, nudging him urgently in the ribs. 'I'm not feeling too well.'

'I know the feeling,' mutters Jub Jub, who is still staring at the pulsating stew in disgust.

'Yes, yes,' mutters Grandad offhandedly, hardly bothering to look my way. 'Probably for the best. Off y' trot to bed then.'

Astonished, I slip silently off my stool. He'd been so very keen for me to stay till the end, to pick up a few 'Slayer tricks', but now, it seems, he's happy for me to just get up and go.

Wondering why this is and what it is he's suddenly hiding, I creep over to the door and pull it ajar...

'Off so soon?' Swiftfist rests a scarred hand on the door, slamming it shut.

A little startled, I nod. If I remember correctly, he'd been sitting by Jagger Steel over by the sink. It seems, then, not only his fist that is swift. 'I'm feeling a bit poorly,' I tell him, pitifully stroking my belly and trying to look pathetic. 'I think I need to sleep it off.'

'But the wiggly worm stew!' he says with an impish glint in his eye. 'A hungry Slayer is not going to stop Grimdorf.'

'I know,' I say evenly. I glance over at Jub Jub who is gawping at his overflowing bowl in horror. 'But I'd rather be hungry than pooping worms.'

He nods, stifling a grizzly grin. 'Wise words.'

'Oh, sorry.' I slap my brow with my palm. 'I forgot to thank you.'

'For?'

'The present you sent me. The binoculars.'

He grins and flaps a dismissive hand at me. 'Forget it. They were yours anyway.'

'They were?'

'Well, sort of. They belonged to Polly, y' mum. I was having a spot of bother with a banshee. The blighter kept hiding in walls so she lent them to me to help me to find him. Very handy, they were. After I slayed him, I planned to return them to her but, well...'

'She was killed.'

He nods soberly.

'Did you know my mum well?' I ask him boldly.

'Oh, yes! And so did Blixt over there. Polly was wonderful. Stubborn, but wonderful; and a fantastically gifted Slayer.'

'Better than you?'

He grins. 'I think she thought so. Look, this spook who reckons your mum didn't slay Grimdorf. Can you trust him?'

I ponder this for a second. Do I trust him? He had been intolerably rude; but, still, my guts tell me he'd been telling the truth, However, this seems a little flimsy, so I say, 'Other spooks told me too.'

'Who?'

'Attila the Hun.'

His eyes narrow. 'Attila the...'

'Hun, yes. Oh, and a mummy, but not a pram-pushing, nappy-changing sort of mummy. A grunting, growling, belongs in a pyramid sort of mummy.' I snap my fingers. 'And I spotted him too,' I suddenly remember, 'lurking by Grandad's tool shed.'

His eyebrows lift. 'I see,' he mutters skeptically. And I can tell from the look he's giving me, he thinks I'm bonkers. 'Tiffany, try not to worry. Tomorrow, when Jagger's, er – sobered up a bit, we'll go and sort Grimdorf for good. OK?'

I nod and lift my chin. 'OK.'

With a crumpled brow, the gnarled Slayer looks at me. 'Tiffany,' he says slowly. 'There's this Scottish saying. If you can't keep up, don't step up. You know, not everybody is cut out to be a Slayer.'

'I didn't step up,' I protest, anger burning in my swift reply. 'It's in my blood. Or so Gramps keeps telling me.'

Puckering his lips, he grunts uncommittedly. I don't think he's a big admirer of my grandad. 'Look,' he says, stepping closer, 'my old dad spent most of his days flipping burgers in a café. My grandad was a cook on a fishing trawler. So it's in my blood to do what? Fry haddock? Deep fry chips?' He puts his hand gently on my shoulder. 'If slaying's not for you, don't do it.'

I chew thoughtfully on my lower lip. Is he right, I wonder. Can I get off this path I'm on?

'After Grimdorf killed your mum and grandmother, we had to find a new Slayer to cover this district. But there was a problem.'

'There always is,' I mutter.

'Devil's Ash is a hotbed of misbehaving spooks. I don't know why, but it is and nobody wanted the job. So we sort of volunteered you.'

'How kind,' I chunter, sullenly.

'Sorry.' He shrugs. 'We hoped...'

'Who's we?'

'Oh, just, you know.'

'No.'

'Well, there's me, Cody Blitz over there and a, er – few others. We form the Slayers' Covern. Anyway, we hoped, with your grandad's help, it's be OK but...'

'He is a help,' I mutter not too convincingly; so, I add, 'A BIG help.'

The Slayer nods slowly. 'Good. Good.' But I can tell he's not fooled. 'Perhaps,' he says with a frown, 'we can send you to Glumweedy's School of...'

'I DO go to school.'

He titters. 'The school I'm thinking of is very different to the school you go to in Devil's Ash.'

'How so?'

He frowns and rubs his grey-flecked whiskers. 'In every way,' he finally says. 'Now, off you trot to, er – bed, was it?'

'Yes,' I say unflinchingly, trying hard not to blink. I find lying very difficult and, in spite of the sunny smile I'm trying to blind him with, I can tell he knows I'm up to no good.

He winks at me. 'Sleep well, then,' he says, tittering in a boyish sort of way. 'And don't worry, I'll tell your grandad to keep a bowl of stew for you.'

'Thanks,' I say with a roll of my eyes. 'Now I'll sleep much better.'

With Boo scampering by my heels, I slip out of the kitchen and hurry down the corridor to the boot closet. After putting on the silk scarf and the pink, sparkly heels I hid there, I softly unbolt the door. 'Stay here, Boo,' I tell the prancing dog. Then, I step out.

There's still no sign of the opera-warbling spook. I wonder, idly, if Grimdorf took her and, if so, why. I sort of miss her now she's not here to turn her back on me. With a shrug, I march up the gravel path. She's no longer my problem. When Grimdorf's history, so am I. After tomorrow, I'm never, ever going to slay another spook.

Then...

GRANDAD'S COTTAGE BLOWS UP!

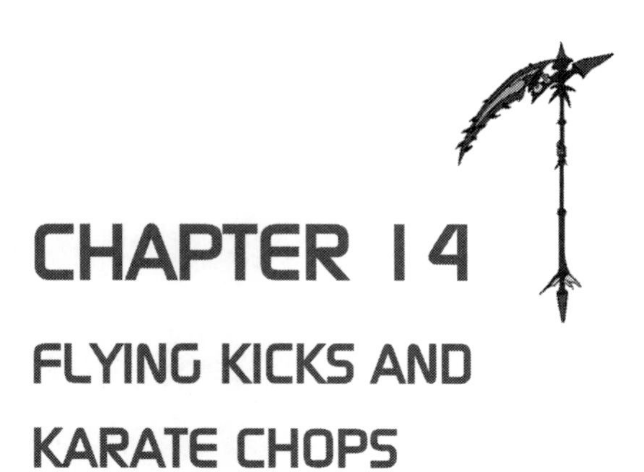

CHAPTER 14

FLYING KICKS AND KARATE CHOPS

FRIGHTENED OUT OF MY WITS, I TUMBLE over and over, landing with a thump in the flower bed. Up to my eyeballs in swaying snapdragons, splinters of wood spill over me, cutting and slicing, scraping my skin. My cheek burns, hot sticky blood dribbling down to my chin.

Then...

Suddenly...

Everything is still.

I try to sit up but the shed's collapsed and the door is lying on my foot. So I just rest there hidden amongst the flowers. Very gently, I finger the torn stem of a snapdragon. It feels so soft and silky. Then I shut my eyes and go to meet my demons.

In a whirl of terror, but knowing I must, I feel my way out from my cosy blanket of sleep to find Boo and the spook from History Class hovering over me.

'How y' feeling, Slayer?'

Gingerly, I put my fingers to my throbbing cheek. 'Skewered,' I mutter.

Sitting up on my elbows, I see my foot is still jammed under the door. Bending my knee, I twist my leg, wriggling my foot to and fro till, finally, it slips free. Shooing Boo away, I struggle to my feet.

In horror, I eye what's left of Grandad's cottage. Most of it is now just a hill of torn timbers and broken piping. I see my bed is now sitting on the top branch of the conker tree and the only surviving thing from the study seems to be the sofa, springs and lumpy stuffing exploding from the cloth. I grit my teeth. The secret room – SLAYER HQ – is now just a smoking crater.

It is a terribly bitter pill to swallow and I tightly shut my eyes. I feel I'm swimming in a river of hurt. A river I remember well...

'Slayer!'

'I'm drowning. DROWNING!

'SLAYER!' yells the boy.

I blink open my eyes and, with a growl, I turn on him. 'Who did this?' I hiss.

'Who do you think?'

Clenching and unclenching my fists, I feel red, hot fury flood my belly. With a snarl, I stagger over to the hill of rubble. 'GRANDAD!' I bellow.

'He's not here,' the boy calls softly. 'Grimdorf pulled him free and took him to Lurch Manor.'

With a challenging scowl, I turn to look at him. 'Rubbish!' I hiss. 'A spook can't pull anybody free from anything.'

'Well, this spook did,' he retorts.

I remember how the yeti lobbed the books at me and the stomping mummy in the canteen. I clench my teeth so hard, it hurts my gums. What the hell is going on? 'Why did he kidnap my grandad?'

'Grimdorf and a few of his spooks looked for you in the rubble. When they didn't find you, he got a bit – upset. So he took the old man. I think he's hoping you will rush up there and try to free him.'

'A trap,' I murmur.

The boy nods. 'A trap.'

My eyes narrow. 'So, you were here then; you saw Grimdorf snatch him.'

'I hid over there.' He flaps a hand at a prickly-looking bush.

'And how did you find me?' I demand, glaring accusingly at him.

'I didn't,' he says with a grin. 'Boo did. He's a very good sniffer dog.'

Scrambling over a shattered chest of drawers, I

discover Swiftfist dabbing his cut knee with a dishcloth, his back resting on a very mangled, upturned kitchen sink.

'You okay?' I ask him, dropping to my knees.

He flaps the bloody dishcloth at me. 'Yes, yes. Just a bit shook up.'

'Where's Cody and the rest of the Slayers?'

Grimly, he thumps the sink. 'They must be under this lot.'

My jaw drops to my chin. 'My God!' I begin to claw at the broken bits of wood. 'Help me!' I cry.

'Don't fret, Tiffany. I'll find 'em. But I'll be needing y' mutt there to help me.'

I nod jerkily. 'Anything.' I turn to Boo. 'Find the Slayers,' I order the prancing dog. 'Go on! Seek! SEEK!'

'BARK!' barks Boo. 'BARK! BARK! BARK!' Then he hovers off, sniffing madly at the rubble.

'I think Grimdorf took Grandad,' I tell Swiftfist, helping him up.

The Slayer's eyes shift to the boy who is still hovering over by the flattened shed. 'Did he tell you?'

'Yes.'

'And was it the boy who told you Grimdorf's back?'

I nod.

Swiftfist sighs. 'Well, he got that right.' Taking hold of my shoulders, the Slayer turns me to face him. 'Go get y' Grandad back. But bring HELL'S TALON with you. Where is it?'

'Grimdorf took it,' I mutter sheepishly, looking to my feet.

I expect him to blow up in anger but all he says is, 'Then you'll be needing this.' I look up to see he is now holding his sword. It is slim and shiny, almost willowy, with a ruby-encrusted gold hilt. I can almost feel the power oozing off it, bewitching me. 'It's called RIP. Legend tells it was forged by goblins in the embers of a volcano.' He offers it to me.

'Thanks,' I say, taking it. The steel seems to glimmer and spark and I half expect it to catch fire.

'I can't go with you; not till I find the rest of the

Slayers. But, when I do, we'll follow you up there.'

I nod my thanks. 'Don't be long,' I tell him. Jumping up, I sprint up the path to the street, but the boy suddenly hovers in front of me, blocking the way.

'I'm sort of in a hurry,' I tell him sternly. 'So shift or I'll slay you with this sword.'

'Step closer,' he says.

I frown. 'Sorry?'

He balloons his cheeks. 'Just do it.'

With a reluctant sigh, I step up to him. Instantly, I'm engulfed in a swirling red mist. The wisps of energy shimmer and glow, ruffling my dress and playing with my curls. His sickly, sweet smell drifts up my nostrils but, oddly, I don't find it repellent. On the contrary! And I fill my lungs with it. 'Wow,' I murmur.

The boy steps away from me and I almost stagger over. Finding my feet, I see I'm no longer on Butchers Street. Now, I'm standing in a long, gloomy tunnel. With a cold chill, I feel a rat scurry over my left foot. If only I had my boots on.

'If we follow this,' the spook says, 'we will end up in the cellar under Lurch Manor. If I was Grimdorf, that's where I'd put your grandad.'

With a gulp, I nod. The cellar is where my grandmother and mum were killed.

With a steely jaw, I begin to jog up the tunnel. It's very dark but it's not a problem. My Slayer blood is pumping and I can see perfectly well.

'Yesterday night,' I pant, 'did you see Grimdorf snatch HELL'S TALON?'

'No.'

His reply is very blunt and I turn to look at him. 'Then where is it?'

The boy shrugs. 'Possibly he took it when I travelled back to 2001 to fetch you.'

I nod slowly. 'Possibly.' The tunnel roof is much lower now so I bend my knees. 'How did he do it? How did he – send me back there?'

'To be honest, I don't know. I can travel through time. All spooks can. Time is, well – nothing to us. There's so much of it, you see. But I don't know how he sent you. I suspect, for just a moment there, he turned you into a spook too.'

I remember how the boy patted Boo, my spook dog. 'So that's why I felt you hand,' I say, feeling oddly embarrassed.

'Yes, I think so.'

'Why did he do it?' I spit angrily. 'Just to hurt me?'

'He's a very powerful spirit. Cunning too. He enjoys a good fight but only if he knows he's going to win. By showing you how potent his magic is, he thinks he'll frighten you off. Is it working?'

'No. I love Devil's Ash. There's no way I'm going to let Grimdorf destroy it.' I stop jogging and turn to him. 'He sent me to the Titanic. When it sunk, a boy drowned. I held his hand; he had tiny fingers.' I swallow, determined not to cry.

'Go on,' the boy says, gently.

'After that, he sent me to war. A man, Spink, got shot. There was blood everywhere. I held his hand too.'

The spook drops lower, his green eyes burning

into me. 'You must try to forget them,' he says soberly.

'But how?' I rest my hands on my knees. 'I so wanted to help them but I didn't know how to.'

'Try to understand, Slayer, Grimdorf simply tossed you into a history book. The final chapters were written. They were beyond anybody's help.'

I nod slowly and carry on jogging, the boy hovering next to me. 'How were you killed?' I suddenly ask him.

For a long second, I don't think he's going to answer. Then, 'I was a pilot in World War Two...'

'A pilot!' I interrupt him. 'But you must be only...'

'Fifteen. When I signed up, I told them I was twenty. The war was going badly and they needed men, so they let it go.'

I nod, remembering Jacob and Spink and how pitifully young they were too.

On July 1st, 1942, I flew a bomber to Germany. On the return leg, we were jumped by a Nazi fighter and the wings were badly shot up. The rest of the crew wanted to jump but I ordered them not to. I wanted to be a hero; fly the bullet-riddled bomber back to Scotland. I almost did it.' He swallows. 'Almost. We crashed in Devil's Ash and everybody was killed but for me.'

'I'm sorry.'

'I only lived for thirteen seconds. But it seemed forever, it hurt so much. I'd killed my crew. I'd killed my crew to try and win a medal.'

I can't think of anything to say so I just keep on jogging, his soft, springy words helping me to keep my mind off the tons of dirt piled up just over the top of my skull.

'I often wonder what I'd do if I was reborn. I know I'd do everything differently. I'd never be selfish; I'd help everybody I meet. Do you think that's silly?'

I frown. He seems so keen for me to understand. 'No,' I say obligingly. 'It's never silly to be kind.'

'You know, I never even kissed a girl. And now, I never will.'

'Oh! Well, can't you kiss a spook. A girl spook.

Or is it just too,' I screw up my nose, 'scabby?'

He snorts. I think he finds my rambling funny. 'Benjamin,' he suddenly says. 'That's my name.'

I twist to look at him. 'Tiffany,' I reply.

At last, the tunnel begins to widen and I find myself in a gigantic cavern lit up by flickering lanterns lining the walls. In the corner, there is a well with a bucket dangling over the abyss, a shovel resting on the low, circular wall.

'Is this the cellar?' I whisper to Benjamin.

He nods, his eyes darting to a set of steps and a door at the top of them, half hidden in the shadows.

I swallow. So this is where Grimdorf killed my mum.

Then...

I spot Grandad!

He is lying on the floor, his left foot shackled to a hoop in the wall.

'Gramps! I hiss. Not wishing to disturb any sleeping spooks, I skulk over to him and drop to my knees. He looks terribly battered – and not in a 'fish and chips' sort of way. His woolly jumper is bloody and torn and there is a deep cut on his chin. But, amazingly, he's still got his slippers on.

Gently, I rest my hand on his craggy cheek.

He stirs, his eyelids flickering open. 'Tiffany!' he gasps, slowly sitting up. 'Coming here is crazy. If Grimdorf spots you, he'll kill you.'

'Not if we scarper,' I tell him brightly, hopping up. I lift the sword and bring it down firmly, slicing the manacle in two. Then I help Grandad to his feet.

'I'm so sorry, Tiffany. I messed up.'

'Don't be silly,' I scold him. 'You were kidnapped by Grimdorf.'

'No, not now. Six years ago. I told your mother and grandmother to go to Lurch Manor and try to slay Grimdorf. I thought, there being two of them, it'd not be a problem.' He looks to his slippered feet. 'I got it horribly wrong.'

With a deep scowl, I say nothing.

'When they didn't return, I went up there to try to find them; to help them. But, I fell over in the forest and twisted my knee.'

'Your limp,' I murmur.

'Yes,' he says miserably. 'Now, every time I walk I'm reminded of how I let them down.'

Suddenly, I feel terribly sorry for him. He'd loved Grandmother and my mum very much and they'd been murdered on his watch. It must be killing him. But he didn't murder them. Grimdorf did.

Tenderly, I nip his cheek, the way he so often nips me. 'Don't worry,' I tell him softly. 'Even Grandads mess up.'

Gripping the old fellow's hand, I help him over to the tunnel. Benjamin, his eyes darting here, there and everywhere, hovers by my elbow. Amazingly, everything is going like clockwork – no sign of Grimdorf and no sign of his mob of monsters – and I wonder why the boy seems so agitated.

'Hold up a sec,' sniffs Grandad, fishing a snotty-looking hanky from his pocket.

'No!' I hiss.

But there's no stopping him and he trumpets

violently into it. The resulting 'BOOM!' ricochets off the cellar walls and, instantly, I feel a shiver of terror run up my spine.

'Sorry,' mutters the old man sheepishly. 'I got a terrible cold.'

A split second later, six oddly-clad spooks zoom down the cellar steps and encircle us.

'Not good,' comments Benjamin in a surprisingly light tone.

Swathed in black with horned helmets and dragon masks, they look like monsters from a horror story. But I can still see the eyes. Stony cold. Killers. Spooks with a job to do. But still, just spooks.

'Ninja,' Grandad mutters darkly, stepping back. I wonder, for a split second, if he's going to try to run for it. But he steps over to the well, picks up the shovel and bucket and together we stand there facing them.

In a flurry of wolfish barks, they charge. I duck under a sweeping sword, twist and elbow my attacker ruthlessly in the stomach. I hit flesh.

Flesh! Just like the yeti. Wheezing, he bends over and I wallop the back of his skull with the hilt of Swiftfist's sword.

Grandad, I see, is still on his feet fending off three of the enemy with the shovel and bucket. I hurry over to help him but then a second ninja jumps me. This fellow is colossal with the stumpy legs of a rhino. His sword sweeps up, grazing the cleft of my chin. I scurry back but he doggedly follows me, jabbing relentlessly for my chest. He is a hunter and he can smell my blood. I block his thrusts and with a howl of fury, I suddenly step up to him and push him up and over the well's low wall. He plummets to the water below.

The swish of steel and I instinctively duck, a shimmering sword skewering the barrel by my shoulder. My third attacker yanks on the hilt trying to wrench it free but it is jammed in the timber.

In the past, I'd do the spook the civility of stepping off; he'd been unlucky and that is no way to win a fight. But not now. Not today. Today,

I cuff him brutally on the jaw.

A volcano spits and growls in my chest, pummeling my rib cage. I see my blurred eyes in the back of the blade, they burn yellow, and fervently I look for the next spook to brawl.

My eyes flit to my grandad. I spot two ninja slumped by his feet but the third is doing considerably better, handling his sword with expert hands. I can tell Grandad is tiring; too much sherry at the Slayers' Dinner.

'THROW THE SWORD.' The demon is back. It knows my instincts, my primal instincts. 'BE ALL YOU CAN BE,' it bellows in my skull. 'THROW IT NOW!'

So I do. I pull the sword from the barrel, the outstretched blade quivering in fury and, with all the venom I can muster, I let fly. It tomahawks over the well, hitting Grandad's attacker with such ferocity, he is thrown twenty feet, landing with a bone-crunching thud on the floor.

With fury simmering under my skin, I storm over to the body. I must...

'YES. YES, YOU MUST.'

...claw open his chest. Gnaw on his ribs.

'DON'T FORGET THE LIVER, LOTS OF IRON IN LIVER. IT WILL KEEP YOU STRONG.'

I must...

'FEED ON HIM!'

I drop to my knees and rip open the ninja's tunic. But then, new words spiral in my mind. Softer. Dampening the fury. They block the demon's playful temptings and, slowly, I slump to the floor.

'Tiffany,' yells Grandad. He limps over to me, dropping to his knees.

'Run,' I whisper. 'Fetch help.'

'But...'

'GO!' I holler.

In a hazy mist, I watch him scamper up the cellar steps.

'Rest now,' the angel tells me, so I do.

CHAPTER 15

FACING GRIMDORF

WITH A NERVY GULP, I LOOK UP TO SEE the most terrifying monster clomping down the cellar steps.

GRIMDORF!

Clothed in a crumpled, moldy-looking tunic and a crooked top hat, he is the most horrifying spook I have ever seen. Taller than Grandad's tool shed, he has jet-black eyes, yellow, bony fingers and teeth the size of a killer shark's. A hissing cat with bent, twisted whiskers stands on his shoulders, his claws digging into the spook's tunic.

With a sort of cowboy-strut, he swaggers over to me, his scythe – MY SCYTHE – clutched in his claw. Still on my knees, I try to scramble away but there's nowhere to go and soon he's standing over me, his rotten lips snarled up in a victory snarl. 'Tiffany Sparrow,' he rasps, stopping and bowing sloppily. I spot the gold buttons on his tunic look old and blotchy and there is a torn cloth patch on his elbow. 'How wonderful to finally meet you.' His tomb-like eyes narrow. 'You remind me so much of your mother.'

'You murdered her,' I boldly hiss back, clambering to my feet.

'Yes.' He nods lazily. 'I did. But, then, she was trying to slay me, A little rude of her, I thought.'

I feel his eyes travelling over me, studying me, sizing me up. Suddenly, I feel horribly dirty and in need of a good scrub. Very, very slowly, I feel for the hilt of my...

'She's going for her sword,' Benjamin calls out.

'What!? Oh, yes.' Grimdorf snaps his fingers

and the sword jumps into his hand. 'Is this Swiftfist's?' he murmurs, studying it. 'Why yes, it is. Excellent!' He stuffs it into his belt next to a silver musket.

I turn and glower at the boy. 'STOP HELPING HIM!' I snarl.

Looking glum, the boy shrugs. 'Sorry Tiffany,' he mutters. In shock, I watch him hover over to Grimdorf. 'I did what you asked,' he says.

Gleefully, the wizard nods and pulls a bottle from his tunic pocket. 'Here's your reward, boy.' Unstoppering it with his teeth, Grimdorf drips three drops of red goo on Benjamin's lips. The boy licks them off then, shutting his eyes, he swallows. With a husky cry, he folds to his knees. He rests there, swaying back and forth, clutching his tummy. Then, suddenly, his chin snaps up, his jaws fly open and he howls.

I don't know what to do. Help him? But it seems he is helping Grimdorf? It seems he is now my enemy?

Suddenly, the boy stops howling. Then, slowly,

he stands up.

Not hovers.

STANDS!

'Be off with y',' growls Grimdorf, his fingers playing with the trigger of the musket on his belt. 'And remember, y' flesh and blood now. Try to cross me and I will shoot you. Got it?'

Benjamin nods and, with faltering steps, he reels drunkenly up the cellar steps.

Enraged, I watch him go. He pretended to help me but it was all just a trick. A trick to get me here – to Lurch Manor. 'WHY?' I yell after him.

He stops and slowly turns to look at me. 'On July 1st, 1942 I messed up. Killed my crew. But now I can put things right.' Gritting his teeth, he yanks open the cellar door and staggers out.

The seconds 'Tick Tock' by in my mind. I can feel my blood pumping and my knees feel juddery and no longer up to the job of holding me up.

Swaying a little, I twist to look at Grimdorf. I must keep the spook talking until Grandad sends help. If he can find any. 'So, what's in the bottle?' I ask him.

The warlock grins horribly, displaying a jumbled row of gigantic, rotten teeth. 'When your mother and grandmother foolishly attempted to slay me here, in Lurch Manor, they were no match for my powers. Even armed with HELL'S TALON, the Scythe of Fafnir.'

I gulp. He knows the legend too.

'But, still, the scythe interested me. Steel embedded with the blood of a dragon cannot simply be discarded or left in the cold hands of a stupid Slayer.'

I feel anger bubbling in my tummy and I grit my teeth. I'm going to get this monster even if it kills me.

'I wished to possess it, Tiffany. Command it to do my will. But, being just a spook, when I went to grab it, it simply slipped through my misty fingers. It was – frustrating.'

'How terrible,' I mock him. 'I think I'm going to cry.'

Grimdorf smirks. 'But I was not to be thwarted. I knew, deep under Bucket O' Blood Cemetery, the blood of the entombed collects. It is hidden in the rock and difficult to find but, I knew, this blood, with a little help from me – a pinch of dragon's horn, a goblet or two of leech pus – if drunk by a spook would bring it back to life. Bring ME back to life. So, I began to drill.'

A lightbulb flickers on in my mind. 'The tremors,' I murmur.

'Yes, admittedly the drilling is a little – risky. And, sadly, the blood I needed was very deep down in the bowels of the planet. But it did not matter. I kept drilling, day and night, until, finally, I was rewarded. I added the leech pus and the dragon's horn and let it brew for six hundred and sixty-six seconds. Then I drank my fill. I know I still look like a spook but, trust me, I'm not.' Gripping the scythe, he lifts it up like a trophy. 'And now I can hold it whenever I wish.'

I step boldly up to him. 'But why would a big, bad warlock like you even need it?'

With a snigger, Grimdorf rubs a bony thumb over the steel. 'Greed,' he says simply. 'A rich man wants only to be richer. Yes, my magic is powerful, but with this blade, I can do anything. Be EVERYTHING! And, so long as I possess it, my army will never defy me. HELL'S TALON – frightens them.'

I remember my nightmare and how the mob of spooks kept bowing to me. It had been so unsettling but, now, I get it. They were never bowing to me; they were bowing to the scythe in my hand.

'But, still, you need this mob of monsters to help you. Why?'

'Slayers,' he growls with venom. 'Too many for even me and the blood of Fafnir to fight. Even the bomb I just put under them will not keep them entombed for long. So I begged my fellow spooks for help. Now they flock to me, keen to drink my brew. I return them to the living world and they, in turn, destroy what I tell them to destroy. And, tomorrow, they will destroy Devil's Ash and any

Slayer who gets in my way.'

'Listen to me,' I beg him. 'You were hung in 1703. Anybody you hurt now, well – they were not even born when you were killed.'

Grimdorf's cold eyes narrow. 'Tell me, Tiffany, do you know why they hung me?'

I swallow, my mind racing. 'For doing magic, I think.'

With a slow, mocking clap, he nods. 'Correct. You know your history. But I did not do it to do evil. On the contrary, I did it to do good; to help a little girl who was dying. Her mother begged me to save her and, foolishly, I did. A tiny spell. Soon she was up and well; and the town, well – they thanked me by stretching my neck.'

'That was then,' I tell him forcibly. 'The world is very different now and so is Devil's Ash.'

'RUBBISH!' he howls, the sheer power of his anger forcing me to back away. 'They will pay for what they did to me. My spooks will torch Devil's Ash till it is just that – ASH!' He pulls the musket off his belt and levels it at me.

Suddenly, I get it. Suddenly, I know how Imelda banished Grimdorf from Devil's Ash. Jessy's words from History Class flood my mind. 'They burnt 'em all,' he'd told the class, 'till they were nothing but charred bone and teeth.' Imelda WAS a witch and she DID put a spell on Grimdorf. But she'd been too frightened to tell Alfred the truth. She'd just seen Rufus Splinter hung for using magic. She didn't want to be burnt or hung too.

'Imelda Cartwright,' I say softly, the wisps of a plan forming in my mind. 'Remember her?'

With the hint of a sneer, Grimdorf slowly lowers his pistol.

'She was a witch, wasn't she?' I press on. 'A very powerful witch and the spell she cast sent you scurrying off in terror.'

The warlock snarls and steps closer.

Stiffening my knees I boldly glower up at him. 'Well, magic runs in the family,' I hiss, brushing my fingers through my red curls. And, with a sly smile, I chant, 'Hocus pocus, diddly...'

With a whiny, Grimdorf cowers to his knees. It

worked! I see my opening and sprint for the steps. Two. Three. Six to go...

BOOM!

On my heels, the third step erupts in a flurry of wood splinters. 'STOP!' Grimdorf yells. But I keep on going. Getting to the door, I yank it open and dash out. I find myself in Lurch Manor, in a long corridor and there, at the very end, I see the front door. Any second now, Grimdorf will be levelling his musket at me so, legs pumping, I go for it.

Almost there.

Almost...

With a howl, the mummy jumps in front of me. But not even a seven foot monster can stop me now. At full pelt, I drop to my knees, slithering between the mummy's legs. Then, I jump to my feet, kick open the door and stumble out into the foggy night.

The sulphury mist is circling me, hiding my enemy, But I know he's out there – hunting for me. I can almost feel him.

I stay perfectly still but for the tip of my scarf which is being whipped up by the wind like a wild puppet on a string. Crossly, I catch it, the only thing I have any control of.

The land judders, the chestnut tree by my elbow swinging to and fro, dropping hundreds of conkers in the long grass. Grimdorf's spooks must still be drilling under Bucket O' Blood Cemetery.

'Where is she?' A yell from within the fog.

The land is no longer juddering; now, it is rocking. But I stay on my feet and slowly back away.

'Don't attempt to run, Slayer,' Grimdorf's mocking tenor puncturing the misty wall. 'Remember the history lesson. You cannot stop me, so why bother to try.'

With a gulp, I backpeddle faster.

FASTER!

FASTER!

'Got you!'

I twirl so fast, I crick my neck. But, still, I'm too slow. With a terrifying growl, the mummy is on me and I'm thrown brutally to my knees.

'Master!' he rasps. 'I captured her. She's over here.'

As if by magic, the swirling mist lifts and I see my tormentor, his cat still hissing and spitting on his shoulder. He strolls over to me, my scythe in his claw, the musket and sword still jammed in his belt. He seems to glow with danger like a stepped-on cobra.

'Good job,' he croons. He slaps the mummy on the back and a puff of dust blooms up. Then he looks to me, a sneer creeping over his torn and bloody lips. 'No chitchat. Let's just do this.' I look on in horror as he lifts the blade...

With a high-pitched whiny, a pony clatters out

of the mist and a boy jumps off, a shovel clutched menacingly in his hands.

'Benjamin!' I cry, struggling away from the mummy's grip and scrambling to my feet.

The boy looks stonily to Grimdorf. 'I grew up on a farm,' he says, his words overflowing with scorn, 'so I know how to kill vermin with a shovel.'

But the warlock just smirks humourously and, with sudden foreboding, I know Benjamin is in deep peril. 'I wonder then,' says Grimdorf, playing idly with the cuff of his shirt, 'if you can duck a bullet too.'

'Stop!' I holler, but the warlock just titters. Then he pulls the musket off his belt and calmly shoots poor Benjamin in the chest.

Sick to my stomach, I sprint over to the boy who is now lying on the grass wriggling in agony. I can tell from all the blood he's in a bad way but there's nothing I can do.

'Just hold on,' I say, pathetically.

I look up to see Grimdorf and the mummy strolling over to me. 'Now, where did we get to?'

says the warlock.

I cower on my knees. 'D - don't kill me,' I splutter. 'I'm only a child.'

Now, I know I'm being a little pathetic but, trust me, if a blood-thirsty skeleton and his rotten-smelling mummy were standing over you, you'd be begging for mercy too.

Grimdorf stops, rocking on his heels. 'I'm not enjoying this,' he tells me coldly. 'It's my job. A cook cooks, a smithy hammers. And my job is to, well, kill Slayers and destroy Devil's Ash. There's no sport in it. No fun.'

'But...'

'Shut up.'

'But...'

'SHUT UP!' He's as unmoving to my pleas as a tombstone.

The mummy puts a bandage-swathed hand on Grimdorf's shoulder. 'Poor Master,' he croons. 'Remember, it is she who is in the wrong for trying to upset your wonderful plan.'

The warlock nods and thumbs the blade. 'Yes, I

know.'

With pot lid eyes, my jaw drops to my chest. Is Grimdorf and his crazy mummy blaming me!? I see thorny-rose red, my blood bubbling in fury. I no longer feel frightened. If I was a viper, I'd be growing fangs and spitting venom. The land seems to feel my temper and shudders too.

'Go on then,' I seethe. 'Stop dilly dallying and kill me. But Swiftfist knows where I am and when I don't return, he'll...'

Suddenly, I stop my rant. The land is no longer rocking. Now it is violently shaking like a jackhammer. With a hiss, the cat jumps to the grass and scampers off. Only feet away, the rock splits, a chasm opening up under my tormentors. With a screech, the mummy plummets into the pit. But Grimdorf is much faster. Casting HELL'S TALON away, he grabs hold of my hand, pulling me with him.

I hover there on the very brink, the top half of my body hanging over the abyss. Beyond the warlock's beseeching eyes I can see a river of bubbling lava. Terror floods me. My feet flap and my free hand claws the dirt, trying to find a hold.

'Let go of me,' I cry. My arm is in so much agony, I'm frightened it will pull free of the socket.

He looks to me, his eyes a sorrowful desert. 'They murdered me,' he says softly, 'for helping a little girl.'

For the shortest of short seconds, I feel sorry for him. Then, I remember my poor mum and my jaw hardens. 'Go to hell,' I yell brutally.

He nods slowly, a shadow blackening his eyes. 'This is only the beginning,' he says.

For a second, I'm frightened he will pull me over too. The world seems to slow as if the machinery helping it to spin is jammed. Then, he lets go of my hand and drops silently into the smoking pit.

Slowly, I pull myself up.

Benjamin whimpers and the memory of the pistol's boom crowds in on me. I scamper over to him. 'Try to stay still,' I tell him, ripping off my scarf and putting it over his bloody chest. 'Help will be here soon.'

But I'm lying and I can tell, from Benjamin's eyes, he knows it. I'm in a forest on a pitch black night. Nobody - NOBODY is going to find us here.

'I-I'm sorry I b-betrayed you,' the boy splutters. He coughs, spraying my scarf with blood. 'I just wanted to – to feel, to do everything over. I let my crew down so badly.'

I grip his hand. 'In the end you stood up to Grimdorf. That took guts.'

'But I was so frightened.'

'To be brave,' I whisper gently, 'you have to be frightened.' I wipe the blood off his chin. Then, very gently, I kiss him. 'Now, let's see if we can think of a way to - Benjamin! BENJAMIN!'

Slowly, his eyes shut and I feel his hand go limp. I choke back a sob and, gently, let go of his fingers. 'I'll miss you,' I murmur. Then I gently kiss his cheek and whisper goodbye.

'I'll miss you too.'

I look up and, for just a second, I see Benjamin hovering over me. He is being greeted by three men in uniform. Then the mist crowds back in and he's lost to me forever.

I sit there. Just – sit there.

The land is still rocking and the crack is still getting bigger. Suddenly, there is a gigantic CRASH! I think Lurch Manor and Grimdorf's mob of monsters just got swallowed up but I can't see for all the mist.

Soon, I know, it will swallow me up too. And, for a second, I'm tempted to let it.

'Run!'

I frown and look back up. 'Benjamin?'

'RUN!'

So, scrambling to my feet, I snatch up HELL'S TALON and leg it.

CHAPTER 16

A BAG OF SOCKS

WHY, I WONDER, DID IT ALWAYS SEEM to drizzle in Scotland on a Sunday. Before setting off this morning, I had put on my mum's old, yellow Mac but tiny, wet droplets still splatter my cheeks and frosty fingers.

It is Christmas Eve and a blanket of mist hangs over Devil's Ash. Everybody seems to be in a hurry, golf umbrellas stabbing eyes and speeding cars splashing unwary shoppers. But I feel oddly detached from it all. My fight with Grimdorf happened almost six months ago. The next day, I went back to Lurch Manor, but there was nothing to see, just a gigantic crater. And, so far, there's been no sign of him returning; or his mob of half-living monsters. But I know he will. Grandad keeps telling me I banished him, but I didn't. The terror in me runs deep and I know he's still out there.

My memory of that horrible night is foggy, a fuzzy mess of grey, blurred drawings. But I remember his words, 'This is only the beginning.' So, for now, my plan to stop slaying is temporarily on hold.

It's not helping that I'm the only Slayer left in Scotland who's still on her feet. Jub Jub lost a leg, Jagger Steel lost six fingers and a thumb and Cody Blitz, well – the poor fellow lost his mind. I think, being trapped under tons of rubble with Grandad's wiggly worm stew was a bit too much for him. Even Swiftfist's not here; he jetted off to a sunny island in the tropics to recover from his injury and he's still not back. I think he's upset I lost his sword. So, with nobody to help me to keep the spooks in check, they seem to be multiplying. FAST! I feel my hands ball up into fists. And I don't know how much longer I can stop them.

On the plus side, Grandad's been wonderful. Even his cooking is getting better! Yesterday, in his mostly bomb-demolished kitchen, he rustled up a pizza; and, no, not with a slug and spider leg topping but with bacon and pepperoni. It was so yummy! He's even been in contact with three Slayers in Peru to see if they will fly over and help me. I hope they do. But, until then, there's just me.

Thankfully, my slaying skills seems to be improving and I'm suffering far fewer cuts and bumps. So much so, Dr Stump now only insists I visit St Crispin's Hospital for a check up every two months and not every two weeks.

I cross the street and splash my way over to a tall, black obelisk sitting only feet from the duck pond. Coming to a stop, I study the silvery words carved into the marble.

In Memory of the Bomber Crew

who Crashed in Devil's Ash

on July 1st, 1942.

They Will Never Grow Old.

Elroy Newell

Arnold Hupman

Harry Hicks

And, there, at the very bottom.

Benjamin Coy

Kneeling in a puddle, I pull a bag of socks from my pocket and set it down in front of the monument. 'There's probably nobody left to remember you now,' I whisper into the cold mist. 'But I do and I always will. I think you were a hero.' I nudge the socks forward with my hand. 'If you bump into a fellow called Spink up there, tell him to put them on. They'll keep his feet dry.'

Glumly, I watch droplets of water splatter the plastic. 'Happy Christmas, Benjamin,' I murmur, clambering to my feet. I rub my wet cheeks, most of the water not having fallen from the sky.

By my boots, Boo whimpers and drools ectoplasmic goo on my foot, his way of comforting me. 'Bark!' he barks. 'Bark! Bark! Bark!' I try to lift my lips to thank him but, sadly, I seem to have forgotten how to.

I often wonder who the angel was who told me to run that night; and who blocked Grimdorf's evil words when I slew the ninja.

My mum.

I think it was my mum.

I burrow my frozen fingers in my armpits to shelter them from the bitter wind. Then with my shoulders hunched, I turn determinedly from the monument and set off on the long, uphill trek back to Grandad's wrecked cottage and the tent in the garden where I now sleep.

Back to slaying unruly spooks.

Back, it seems, to what I was born to do.

The Boy Who Piddled In His Grandad's Slippers

Words by Billy Bob Buttons Drawings by Lorna Murphy